'*Solomon's Seal* is a brave collect[ion] [...]
sexual grief and family life. [...]
romantic, and strangely adult, a[...]
after a long lifetime of letters. [...] [...]ained in
seamless prose. She even succee[...] [...]king loneliness sound
homely, and yet few writers have penned frustration with such
accuracy. You cannot mistake her for anyone else'

DERMOT HEALY

'A taut melancholy wires its way through the stories of *Solomon's
Seal* ... McCloskey writes with a haunting certainty ... the stories
build their memorable world cumulatively, piece by brittle
affecting piece' THE TIMES

'It's a pleasure to welcome the advent of a poised, fluid and
darkly memorable voice in Molly McCloskey, an author capable
of capturing and compressing the most vivid imaginative worlds
within these compact, haunting stories' DERMOT BOLGER

Molly McCloskey was born in Philadelphia in 1964, and moved to County Sligo in 1989. She was awarded the RTE/Francis MacManus Award in 1995 and her stories have been published in *London Magazine, Phoenix Irish Short Stories 1996,* and broadcast on BBC Radio.

Solomon's Seal
and other stories

MOLLY McCLOSKEY

PHŒNIX

A Phoenix Paperback
First published in Great Britain by Phoenix House in 1997
This paperback edition published in 1998 by Phoenix,
a division of Orion Books Ltd,
Orion House, 5 Upper St Martin's Lane,
London WC2H 9EA

The author would like to acknowledge the support of the
Arts Council of Ireland. She would also like to give special thanks
to Martin Healy.

'The Wedding Day', 'Diamonds' and 'You Used To Be My
Mother' were first published in *Force 10*. 'The Stranger' was first
published in the *Fish Anthology*, a volume of prize-winning stories
from a competition run by Fish Publishing, County Cork. 'Death
of a Salesman's Wife' was published in *Cyphers*. 'Mythology' was
published in *Irish Short Stories* (Phoenix House, 1996). 'Solomon's
Seal' was first published in *London Magazine*. 'Family Photos',
'Hands' and 'Losing Claire' were broadcast on RTE Radio.

A CIP catalogue record for this book
is available from the British Library.

ISBN: 0 75380 139 6

Printed and bound in Great Britain by
The Guernsey Press Co. Ltd,
Guernsey, Channel Islands

For Neets

Contents

Solomon's Seal

I was nineteen when I first learned that my father was not really my father. It was the summer he turned forty. The last summer I lived with him in the house on Pilkington Road. We lived alone there because my mother had died when I was an infant, leaving us in one another's hands.

My father's passion in life was the garden. He especially loved his roses which twisted on their lattices up the sides of the house, curling and dropping over the doorframes like thick locks of hair.

When I was very young, he introduced me to this first love of his, assigning to me the simplest tasks, like scattering seed over ground he had prepared, or weeding, which I only had to do until I got bored and began to daydream. Then I was left to spend the day blowing motes of dandelions into space, or stroking the moss which grew in soft tubes between the terraced brick and reminded me happily of caterpillars.

Later, he gave me more complex lessons. The precise methods and months of pruning, techniques of grafting, creating the illusion of decadence according to a plan. The lessons stayed with me, so that the things that remind me of him still are the most pleasing things. The smells of cut grass and of roses, the first buds in spring, burning in the autumn, towers of pots teetering in garden sheds. Simple tools like trowels and spades and hoes.

★

My mother died when I was two and she was twenty-three, not long after my grandmother's death. Cousins of hers had invited her to go sailing on the bay, hoping to take her mind off the difficult period that had just ended. She had nursed her mother through a long bout of pneumonia when they discovered that the older woman had developed cancer of the bone. Mother was with her for much of that year, staying at her house for weeks at a time. The death had left her physically exhausted, and she was looking forward to a day away from it all. Away from us even, my father had said. Out on the water, which she loved just as he loved the soil.

The morning was sunny and calm but a storm blew up after lunch. It was never clear why they were unable to navigate their way through waters which, to competent sailors, should not have been fatal. When the boat was found, there was a large gash in the hull. The damage occurred either somewhere in the bay, which was peppered with rocks – though they were well mapped – or outside the bay, where the boat was eventually swept.

All we were sure of was that the three of them drowned. That while my father and I played a clumsy, delightful version of marbles on the living-room floor of our cousins' beach house, they were drowning.

My father was devastated. In the three years he had known my mother he'd worshipped her, and her sudden and early death prevented her from ever becoming ugly to him, or from ever disappointing him. She was never debased or falsely exalted by having to listen to any lies, she never smelled other women on his fingers or on his breath or in his hair, and she never poisoned the air between them by ushering in untruths of her own.

She remained frozen. As frozen as her image in a

photograph taken only days before her death. Dark glasses and a scarf tied beneath her chin. It was taken on the deck of that same beach house. Cocktail hour. She is sitting in a patio chair with a drink on the table beside her, her head thrown ever so slightly back, her smile flashing at someone just to the left of the camera. There's no one else in the picture, just my mother, alive, her eyes hidden, the bad times seemingly behind her.

It was my father's favourite photograph. It captured the essence not only of her – at her most beautiful and promising and defiant – but of him as well. That was the apex of their lives together – that brief time between tragedies – and it became for him a repository in which he stored all of the faith of his youth, but to which he would never again have access.

There were other women, I'm sure, in his life after that, though I was unaware of them as a child. He never brought a women home, and of his occasional outings he didn't speak. As I grew older I understood that whatever affairs he had were conducted elsewhere, presumably to shield me from hurt, possibly because he never met anyone he considered suitable to make a part of our home. As for me, I was relieved at not ever having to welcome intruders into the house, the way friends I knew were forced to do, smiling sweetly at the odd romantic interests of their divorced or widowed parents. I never had to look at women's bodies, and wonder what my father knew of them, and where this left the memory of my mother.

I never really pined for a mother, either, because I didn't remember having one. I loved my father and he gave me all that he could, of himself and of life. Far more than the fathers of my friends gave to them, and this made up for whatever jealousies or emptiness I might've felt.

He doted on me in much the same way that he did her memory. Together we covered every inch of childhood, and all of its perfectly rendered events and activities are etched in my mind. Swingsets, circuses, rides on ponies while he held my hand, Sunday matinées of the latest animated films, the *Nutcracker* at Christmastime, painted eggs at Easter. He didn't spoil me – there were strict bedtimes, careful monitoring of schoolwork and precisely enforced codes of conduct. He just did his best to ensure that my young life was fleshed out. And I had no reason to believe that there was anything less than blood in our devotion to one another.

I learned of it by accident, and in the way we learn of so many secrets which predate us: through letters. For brief periods in 1958, while she was nursing my grandmother, my mother was apart from my father and me. She wrote to him almost daily before her death and he kept the letters, locked in the drawer of a large roll-top desk in his study.

Despite its always being locked, the drawer itself had never held much interest for me. I assumed it to be full of official and uninteresting documents, perhaps the draft of a will, birth certificates or a life insurance policy.

He must've been reading the letters the previous night, because he was late going up to bed and had been in the study most of the evening. When he'd closed the drawer, he'd left the key in the hole. As I said, I'd never had more than a passing regard for the drawer's contents, but when I saw the following day that I could satisfy a mild curiosity once and for all, and without going to any trouble, it seemed natural to do so.

Most of the letters related the ways in which my grandmother was deteriorating, how the two of them spent their days, the weather, their meals, some car trouble my mother had had or a book she was reading. Others contained no news at all, simply declarations of love and devotion. References to *when all this is over, and we can get on with our lives.* She wasn't being hard-hearted. She just missed her husband and her baby and wanted out of that painful limbo. A handful referred specifically to me:

I am beginning to think, she wrote, *that, despite what we agreed, we shouldn't tell her. She is growing to love you like a father and a father is what you've been and will be for her, I know. By the time she's old enough to understand, the adjustment will be too great.*

In another she had written, *I don't want her searching for him. That never comes to any good.*

It was obvious that he was writing back to her, and sometimes arguing this point. He believed I should be told the truth, that searching or not should be my decision when I was old enough to make it. He felt uncomfortable about living a lie. If I loved him, that was fine, but he wanted me to love him within the limits of who he really was.

That evening, I sat waiting for him on the small patio which opened off our kitchen and looked out over the garden, which the two of us had so often tended side by side. He was whistling when he came in the front door, unaware that I was there. He set a big brown bag of groceries on the kitchen table and began unpacking it, his tanned arms dipping in and out of the bag, his expression relaxed and satisfied. When he was finished, he folded the bag neatly and put it away and then got himself a bottle of beer. Tilting back his head to take a long swallow, he saw me, and raised his hand cheerfully in greeting. We had always been happy to see one another.

As he walked to the patio door, he unbuttoned the top button of his shirt and pulled from side to side on his necktie. Then he leaned on the doorjamb, surveyed the blank blue sky, and said, 'God, another beautiful day.'

I didn't answer, just looked at him.

'What is it?' he said, looking straight back at me, worried.

'I know,' was all I said.

There was only one way I could've come upon the information, and so he didn't question how I had. Instead, he crossed his arms over his chest, squinted out across the back yard and then slowly lowered his gaze to the ground in front of him. Finally, he sat down beside me on a wicker chair and locked his hands together around the bottle. Still looking at the ground, he said to me, 'Your mother was pregnant with you when we met.' And then he stopped.

'Go on,' I said.

'She told me that right at the start.'

'Go on,' I said again, more insistent.

'She didn't want me to think she was trying to trap me. Your mother wasn't like that. She was quite prepared to raise you on her own. But ... we fell in love.'

'What happened to him?' I asked.

'I don't know. And she didn't either. It was just ... something that happened.'

'*Something that happened.*'

'You know I didn't mean it that way,' he said quickly.

'He left because she was pregnant?'

'No,' he shook his head. 'He never knew. He was gone before she even knew.'

'Gone where?'

'I don't know. He was only here temporarily, six weeks or something. Setting up an office in town, if I remember.'

'And she never tried to contact him?' I asked, in disbelief.

'I can't say what it was like for her. All I know is what she told me.' He looked away from me then and rolled the bottle between his palms.

'Well?'

'Well … '

'What did she tell you?'

'She told me,' he said slowly, 'that he wouldn't have wanted to know. And, anyway, she didn't want him a part of her life.'

'Why? What was wrong with him?'

'Nothing. It's just that there wasn't anything between them. She didn't love him.'

'She loved him enough,' I said.

'No,' he said firmly. 'She didn't.'

Then he sat there in silence, his elbows on his knees, unable to look at me, scowling at something in the distance. Angry with my mother for the first time in seventeen years, for having left him to explain.

'I had intended to tell you,' he started again, 'but when she died … I couldn't do it on my own. You depended on me so much. And of course,' he shrugged, 'I would've had no idea where to find the man.'

'You could've tracked him down, though. If he'd worked in town … '

He bit his lip and still wouldn't look at me.

'Three years had passed … ' he said quietly.

I knew then why he'd never tried. For my mother's sake, for my sake, but mostly for his own. He'd wanted to keep me. I was her blood, his most intimate connection with her, and he'd grown to love me.

But now there was this other man, frozen too, just like my mother. I could nearly see him. He wore a dark suit and tie, and a starched white shirt. A briefcase swung for ever from his hand. He was clean cut, heading towards his car at the end of the day, one of those pure white, 1950s' smiles flashing on his face. Setting up an office, screwing my mother, leaving his seed in her.

I wasn't as shocked as I might've been. In hindsight, my relationship with my 'father' had always seemed out of the ordinary. In raising me, he had acted not as though I belonged to him, but as though we were stealing precious time together. I believe that he never got over the fear that one day a stranger would appear to reclaim me, and he would be revealed as the fraud that he was.

For a time, our lives went on as usual. I was not interested in searching for my real father. The idea frightened me more than anything. It was like my mother had written: It seldom came to any good. And, after having lost her, I was anxious to hold on to what I had, and what I knew, which was the man who'd raised me. My love for him seemed stronger than ever, now that I knew why he'd raised me, and in the fashion that he had. And I felt his love for me as different too because, to some degree, it had been given by choice. But also because I had commanded it.

So, for a short time, the knowledge transformed us only for the better. Our most banal exchanges seemed infused with something just short of awe. He watched me first with fear, and then relief, as he realized I wouldn't leave him. And I, detecting no sign of his devotion to me having lessened, felt a deepened trust in him. We were like any two people who suddenly share a great and extravagant secret. We looked at one another as though we couldn't quite believe it. Or as though we were newly wed.

Gradually, however, strange nuances crept into our behaviour. We began skulking about, as though guilty of something. He found reasons to be away from home at night; I didn't sunbathe in the garden. Our casual touches – a hand on an arm in laughter, the grip and squeeze of shoulders from behind, gentle slaps of feigned displeasure – all ceased. Our eyes darted into corners and, when our backs were turned, we shot furtive glances at one another. For the first time in my life, I wondered where he'd gone at night over the years. I thought, as I never had before, of other women's bodies he might've touched, or was touching then.

One night I came home and found him asleep in the living-room chair. I could tell by the caught, exaggerated sound of his breathing that he had been drinking. He had never been a heavy drinker, though I'd certainly seen him drunk on occasion, and he'd always been pleasant and goofy and slightly maudlin. But drinking alone was not like him, and it was clear that he had been doing just that all evening. I lay down on the sofa and watched him. The heaving of his chest and stomach, the way his strong legs were splayed so that the space between them formed a diamond. The dark, thinning thatch of hair, cut short and boyish, and the heaviness of his beard at that hour of the night, the feel of which I knew from when we'd embraced on important or happy occasions.

I watched him until my sight grew glassy and his familiar form began to flicker, like the first tics of dreaming. Eventually, I fell asleep myself. By the time I woke, it was light out and he had gone to work. I spent that day wandering aimlessly about the house. I picked up discarded items of his, of mine, and returned them to their proper places. I cut larkspur. I sat in his study, spinning idly in his leather chair. I smelled him.

When he returned home in the evening, he was edgier

even than he had been, and avoided my eyes. He fixed himself a drink and didn't speak, turning his broad back to me, his free hand gripping the edge of the counter top. I stood across the kitchen from him, chopping vegetables for dinner, waiting for him to face me. He did. For the first time in weeks we looked squarely at one another. My father's eyes were brown, like his hair, and his face and arms a lighter brown, from hours spent in his beloved garden. Gold hairs shone against his skin. I could hear his breathing becoming more pronounced. His jaw set and I saw the other features of his face tighten slightly, as though he were in pain, but bearing it. I knew then that he had watched me as I slept, just as I had watched him.

'Come here,' he said to me, and held out his hands.

We touched clumsily at first, used only to brushing one another's cheeks, and then chastely, shyly disengaging. But soon we were kissing hungrily and without shame, his face scraping against my jaw, down along the line of my neck, his hands like a vice on my skull, trying to pull me further into him.

Though he was passionate and feverish and whispered my name with what sounded like rapture, he never smiled or showed any of the other simpler signs of pleasure.

In the morning, he sat dressed on the edge of the bed and told me he was terribly sorry.

As I knew he would, he worked in the garden that day. I watched him stooping among the many flowers we had planted. Columbines, irises, Solomon's seal. Lobelia, spilling like a purple stream over a shelf of rocks. He worked without gloves. He used to say that there were things in the soil – minerals – that, when in contact with human skin, calmed the mind.

At lunchtime, I brought him a sandwich and a glass of

cold tea. He looked at me wistfully, and with sorrow, and it seemed that any joy I had ever brought him had been swept from his memory. That, instead, I resembled the embodiment of all the small and various failings of his life. Every time he'd ever fallen short. And while I longed to tell him that it hadn't been wrong, to comfort him and to touch the places on his body which were now dear and known to me, I knew I couldn't.

Neither could I join him at his work. In these immediate and hateful ways, things had changed between us, and so, for the rest of that afternoon, I sat at the upstairs window, cut off from him, watching him. From time to time he would stop what he was doing and lean his forearm on the handle of the tall shovel, or, if he was kneeling, rest his knees in the dirt and, with his palms pushing on his thighs, stare into the distance.

The following week we went about our separate lives, saying only what was necessary, seeing as little of each other as was possible. My father worked long hours and I prepared for my September departure to the university. On one other occasion we were lovers.

We had been at a lawn party up the street – some neighbours we'd had for years were moving away. We stayed all afternoon and well into the evening and had both drunk more than we were accustomed to. On the long walk down Pilkington Road we felt, in the air's sweet perspiration, the first hint of autumn on our faces. Though he found it sad, or perhaps because he did, it was my father's favourite season. I knew that soon after I left he would light small bonfires, burning what he'd cut back, filling the air with the sharp grey smoke of autumn. That he would do alone what for years I'd helped him do. I knew how the bright berries of the firethorn would catch his eye, the sprays of montbretia, the short gold evenings, and I ached to stay with him.

When we turned into our drive, he put his arm around me and I leaned into the hollow underneath his shoulder. I thought nothing of his gesture, so adamant had he been to put what we'd done behind us. We'd often walked this way in the past, innocently, and in the warm fluid space that was my thoughts, I welcomed our return to one another.

When we got inside the house, we spoke briefly at the bottom of the stairs about what a lovely day it had been and how tired we both were. We embraced as we had so many times before, and as we had not dared to do since that day. But our bodies had developed something beyond us, a language beyond our thoughts and conscious wishes. Our goodnight embrace became a kiss and, in the dark of the hallway, we sought one another again.

In the days that followed, my father slipped into an almost morose silence. He seemed haunted and depressed, and once again stayed away from home as much as he could. Only once did I catch him looking at me, and it was with despair and resignation.

On the morning of my departure, he was up early, making a breakfast, helping me with my bags and last-minute preparations. He drove me to the station, occasionally taking my hand and squeezing it between his, but keeping his eyes always on the road. I looked mostly out the window and cried as quietly as I could. I was going two hundred miles away from him, away from our home and the garden we had kept and the bed we'd slept in.

At the station, we sat on a hard wooden bench waiting for the train. My father held my hand again, and again told me that he was sorry, and that he'd been wrong. He said he loved me just as he always had and that whenever I needed anything, I should call him. He said he hoped we could get over what had happened. He called me his daughter.

When the train came we embraced, at first tentatively, and then tightly. His face was wet with my tears and I could feel the short stiffness of his hair and all the contours of his body pressing and moulding to my own. My eyes were shut and in the darkness there was no sense of time, or of where we were, and I imagined never letting him go, and the joy of that. But he stepped away from me and, holding his hand fast to the back of my skull, the way he once had, he looked at me. I waited for him to say something, but he couldn't speak. Tears were in his eyes as well, and soon I turned away from him and boarded the train.

During my first semester at the university, I went home some weekends just as the others did, and again at Christmas. But, already, my brief experience of the world beyond home had changed me. A sadness dogged us, and a combination of longing and shame drifted between us. We could take pleasure in none of the things we once had, not the garden or cooking a dinner or even conversation, and I found myself sitting in the empty house or, if he was at home, going out to visit old friends in whom I had little interest.

Without either of us suggesting it, I gradually stopped coming home, and that summer found myself a job in the town where the school was situated. We continued to write, as that never caused the same degree of pain, and as we were loath to really let go of one another, having had years of happiness just that side of my departure.

When I finished school and moved further west, we

wrote less and less. But we kept each other informed of the bare bones of our lives, and so I knew that he still lived in the house, still worked and had never remarried. Once a year I would arrange to see him, and we would meet at some neutral location halfway between our homes. For a time, certainly, I felt some of the horror which my father had felt during my last days with him, and to which I had been immune. But that feeling abated, as the uneasy desire had, and in time our meetings lengthened and became a great source of comfort to us. We talked about our lives and our work, in the way that other fathers and daughters do. I enquired about the garden, and he described to me the herbs and vegetables which were slowly gaining ground on his beloved flowers – a growing streak of practicality which he attributed to age. Often, we laughed. The one thing we never spoke of was that summer.

Over the years, I watched his face grow lined, the skin of his neck slackening, the slowing of his gait. I watched him harden into his aloneness, so that his life seemed a shell to me, protecting the softer bits of him I knew to be inside. In the end, I felt nothing but love for him because of the ways in which he had never changed.

Apparently, at the time of his death, there was no woman in his life. At the funeral, no one stood out among his acquaintances and colleagues as having been special to him. Possibly he had never been truly happy with a woman since my mother's death, and in that regard, I had brought him nothing but pain. But I mourned him properly, threw roses and a handful of soil from his own garden into the grave, and cried for him like the lover that I was.

The Wedding Day

At the worst of times, my family is nothing more than a shared set of circumstances to which there is no agreed-upon response. But I prefer to think of us as individuals. As connected by something more, if only an obsessive desire for uniqueness amidst the distorted mirror images to whom we are bound until death: each other.

We all lost religion together, though naturally at different ages. For some strange reason – strange because I don't believe in God – I see that as the turning point. If I could choose one image to represent us, it is of seven strings unravelling simultaneously from a great ball, until there is only an empty space left where the core used to be.

At the same time, we seem almost desperate to get away from one another, but this I take as proof positive that the ties are unbearably strong. In truth, we are afraid of them. We are afraid of our *selves* being swallowed up, consumed by common pasts we can't fully recall and secrets we never chose to share. We try to scream our aloneness, which is, of course, a pathetic attempt at the impossible.

At family reunions, we feel like soldiers returning from a tour of duty.

I was sitting in the outer portion of Larry's quarters on an unusually humid day. Death and trapped heat sucked all the fresh air from the room, and the long red crushed-velvet curtains reminded me of a cheap brothel in a movie. The bedroom, which I had just left, was littered with Larry's dirty ashtrays. There were two photos taped to the wall – one of Gandhi and one of Jerry Garcia. A worn raincoat hung from the top corner of the closet door. If a stranger had walked in, he would have had little idea who Larry had been.

Mother and Father were sitting either side of the bed, heads hanging limply from their necks, like flowerheads snapping their stems. The current of failure that ran between them was palpable. It pushed me from the room.

I say *quarters* because home would be too cosy a term. Larry was placed there by the state when his former facility was knocked down to make way for an exclusive riverfront development. It was considered prime property, and a pity to be wasting on twenty-odd oddballs who didn't appreciate the view.

I had never seen a dead person before, let alone a man caught in the act of dying. I had never been to a viewing and seen someone all starched and stitched up and smiling. I think it would make me vomit to look at that. I much preferred this. A dying man who looked like hell.

It was a matter of sitting it out. I had plenty of newspapers with me, but the light wasn't great. Besides, I felt guilty for trying to take my mind off an event on which I should've been dwelling. How often will my brother die? I thought. Only once, and he deserves my undivided attention when he does.

The doctor said Larry wouldn't live through the night. He said it very matter-of-factly, just like that: He won't live through the night. I think he felt it would be a relief to us. Larry had been off his lithium – his lifeline – for three days because the shift nurse had failed to make her rounds. On the third day, he wandered out into traffic and left some poor soul with a guilty conscience that will most likely put happiness forever out of reach. You might think it odd that I worry about the guy who hit him rather than about my brother. But my brother's life was effectively over twenty years ago.

I poked my head round the door. I'm going for coffee, I said.

Larry was dead by the time I got back. He was forty-five.

We last came together as live entities on 27 August 1988, in a small house opening onto the Atlantic Ocean. The eve of my only sister's wedding. A late summer breeze wandered in through the open double doors, lending an untrue lightness to the room. We were all very busy acting nonchalant, pretending not to notice our excitement. We are a jealous lot.

Georgie was on his fifth vodka, another thing we pretended to ignore. Mother was trying to roll pieces of roast beef and turkey into quaint little sandwich-sized cylinders, but the thin slices kept cracking and leaving her with messy strands that amounted to nothing.

Jay was feeding his youngest daughter from a bottle while his wife slept, and Sabina, the bride-to-be, was engrossed in an article in *Sports Illustrated* about the Chicago Bears. I was sipping a sweating beer and watching Larry's back as he sat perfectly still on the deck.

Father was absent, wouldn't arrive until the morning of the wedding. He still appears at the big events, like a celebrity emcee. He is the master of the cameo, hovering about the perimeter of our less-than-perfect circle, waiting for just the right moment to make his entrance. He's always had an inkling that he's missing something but, poor man, he is never sure exactly what it is. It's natural. How could anyone attend so many birthdays and not wonder what happens in between?

That morning, I'd read a story in a magazine about fear and demons and how family can keep them both at bay. But that was somebody else's solution. For us, every time we turn our heads or avert our eyes, the demons close in. They are the truth, insofar as we perceive it. That's the problem with families. We feel too much about each other, so we can never look directly into one another's eyes.

Sabina must be altogether enveloped in fear right now, as she pretends to read about the Bears.

It was their second 'upset' of the season, she says. I told you, Jay, you should've asked for my advice before you signed up for that pool at your office.

The baby gurgles and milk runs down her chin. Jay looks sideways at Sabina, who can't see that he has bigger things than football on his mind. But what's really on his mind is the fact that his sister's knowledge of the game is greater than his own. I have little on my mind except Larry. At least he is smart enough to turn his back when not looking us in the eyes.

She was always so cool — Sabina, I mean — that I could never quite catch up with her. It was like following a fashion that forever eluded me. And now, here she was, stepping blithely off the deep end of life, one foot in the grave, the other laced snugly into her pink Converse hi-tops, not a trace of fear in that sublime smile of hers. But it has to be there. It's one of those things family can feel.

I often wonder why she likes me so much. I suspect I must be a lot of things she looks down on, not the sister she would've chosen. I have always felt rather frivolous in her presence. She is balanced and straightforward and very happy, whereas I tend to reel from one extreme to the other, like a drunk being pushed around in a crowd. I try to return what Sabina feels for me, but it seems I never really can. My twitches of envy and admiration, coupled with the intermittent empathy we feel for people whose ships are sinking alongside our own, are not the same.

So where was she when Larry died? Well, she was with Georgie, trying to persuade him that he should, at the very least, come to see his brother off. But Georgie said: There's too much old baggage between us. If I show up, he'll know he's going to die. If I don't, well, who knows?

I think he loved Larry. And I actually believed what he said. But Sabina thought it was bullshit and she said so. She speaks to him now and they mock one another like always, but things will never be the same between them. She blames him for something, though it cannot logically be Larry's death.

We wallow in blame. It's one big circle of blame. For what we've become, for what we haven't become. We play tag with our blame, only now all of our running and chasing is inside our own heads, instead of out on the big green lawn behind our house.

I escape for a while. The six bodies in that room with their silent screams for attention are too much for me. I walk to the mini-market for a magazine or cigarettes or anything. It is just dusk. The eve of my only sister's wedding. She has made another wonderful choice in life. It is obvious to everyone.

How does this make me feel? Sad? Definitely. Left out? A touch. Proud? Undoubtedly. She is blood, you know, and all blame and envy aside, I am incurably proud of her.

It is four p.m. on the wedding day. The sun is soft and drained of strength, the way late summer sun can be. The few people left on the beach are admiring us and their children are pointing. Who can help but blush before a bride and groom? They are a lot like children themselves, with their innocence and their blind faith. They lend us their hopes, even when they are strangers.

Before Sabina and John have exchanged I dos, Larry begins to clap and then to giggle. Those in the small ceremony who don't know us that well look embarrassed, but they smile that smile that means: We can rise above these little catastrophes, he's one of God's children too. Mother squeezes Larry's arm to reassure him and touches her head to his shoulder. She is his best friend.

Sabina feels betrayed. She encouraged Larry to come, though he didn't want to. He doesn't like crowds, crowds full of normal people who know when and when not to clap. But he is her blood, and she is who she is, so she smiles.

Father is carefully inspecting his shoes as the ceremony continues. I suspect it is because he feels moved or sad or elated. But then I always was a romantic – attributing tender, tragic emotions to people when what they're really thinking about is dinner or the new secretary with the nice breasts or the mounting pressure in their bladders.

But this time I am right. When he looks up the struggle is apparent. He is of the old school – which, it seems, is still pumping out graduates – where they teach men not to cry. He surveys his family one by one, beginning with Sabina, his pride and joy. The girl he drove to piano lessons. The girl he took shopping for her first bikini. The girl he is giving away.

He loves Georgie, in a back-slapping, comeradely kind of way. This strange, utterly male exuberance bursts forth when they greet one another. It excludes me, but I don't mind. I am happy for them, or try to be. Larry is a different story, of course. First-born son and all those lost years. I look away when my turn comes and try to sport a serious profile for my father's benefit.

The great wide chasm in his life is opening up before him. He's not stupid, but he's bargained away a lot, and at times like this he wonders if he made the biggest blunder of his life. He wonders where all those innocent, faith-filled hopes of his and Mother's slunk off to. For slink they did. There was nothing noble about it.

All of a sudden, everyone around me is chattering and laughing. I've missed the kiss because I was looking at my father looking at Jay. Jay, who was standing at perfect attention, holding his pretty wife's hand and looking every inch the highly successful computer analyst and family man that he was. He had it all sewn up and Dad was looking at him.

Two years later, while Jay was watching his wife do the dishes, he decided he didn't love her any more. At least this is what he told me. The penny dropped, and dropped and dropped, with each sparkling, lemon-scented plate she placed on the drainboard. Now they have their own set of strings unravelling from their own once tightly wound core.

Was anybody happy? Failure loves company but, really, I couldn't go so far as to say we ever smiled on one another's misfortunes. We may be jealous but we're not vicious. I know the real reason Georgie didn't go to his brother's deathbed and I did. Me, who hardly even knew him. He was telling the truth, only Sabina didn't believe him because he wasn't speaking her language.

When Georgie said, There's too much old baggage between us, he meant that he couldn't separate the love from the hate. And, anyway, how the hell was he expected to go through life with the image of his first idol expiring in a yellowed bed of insanity and delirium? He has his own sanity to think about. But Georgie graduated from the old school, too, so he just said, No, and we all thought, What a cold bastard.

Likewise, when Jay concluded while watching his wife stacking dishes in their oak-panelled, purpose-built kitchen that he didn't love her any more, what he really meant was: I'm getting older. I need something more than I've agreed upon. I'm panicking.

Sabina and John haven't panicked yet. Somehow, they've managed to stave off the threats to their stability and their sanity. We are all pulling for them. But if they fail, if the rug goes out from under them and they suddenly find themselves lonely and casting strange glances around at cocktail parties, we won't be surprised.

The Stranger

When Frederick turned thirty-eight he realized he was fat. Not too fat, but not like he was, not like before, when he didn't think about things like a second piece of pie or the apparent flatness of other men's stomachs. It was sudden, like he'd reached the age where things like that just snowball. He joined a gym, but he doesn't often go because most of the men there are young and thin and confident, like those with whom he's been doing business recently. When he makes love to his wife, gravity pushes his belly downward into the hollow of her stomach. And if he lies on his back, it seems to spread out on all sides, and he is ashamed for her to see him. In the mornings, he pulls the sheet up to his chest as if he is afraid, or else hurries to the shower before she is awake.

Funny thing is, for all Frederick's furtive eating and more furtive love-making, the few pounds he has put on have never caught his wife's attention. Used to be, Julia lay back at night, watching possessively as Frederick loosened his tie, slowly unbuttoned his dress shirt and draped his trousers carefully along the creases. But one evening, Julia fell asleep before he even had his shoes off, and it was months before either of them noticed that anything had changed.

Frederick is still in love with his wife. When she wears a certain red dress that holds her body like a lover, he feels shy with admiration. He likes her company, the way she stands at the kitchen counter and reads novels with the radio playing and the complicated dinner cooking. The way she is warm and languid like a cat and purrs goodbye at him from under the covers in the mornings.

But lately, at home in the evenings, Frederick has been given to fits of crying. Part of this strange snowballing loss of control he feels. He locks himself in the bathroom and sits on the side of the olive-coloured tub, with his elbows on his knees. He gently knocks his forehead against his palms, whispering, What is wrong with me? What the hell is wrong with me? His only comfort is that Julia hasn't noticed.

Frederick stumbles into it. He isn't the sort of man who chases women, and often he is not the sort of man who notices when women are chasing him.

You mean you haven't noticed? his workmates say.

Freddie ... the way she looks at you ... the one from upstairs ...

Oh, says another, the one who's always looking for raisins at the salad bar?

Sheila, I think, says a third.

Hunh-uh, says the first, I'm talking about the other one. The blonde.

It isn't Sheila, or the blonde from upstairs, or the raisin lover who Frederick stumbles in with. It is a woman named Beth who arrives in his advertising agency one day, looking for a new way to talk about telephones. Examining a sketch over his shoulder, she smiles at everything he says and decides she likes his smell. That evening when they are having a drink, he sits perpendicular to her at the corner of the bar. By arranging himself so, he is preserving the illusion that nothing is going on. But after two drinks, Beth puts her hand on Frederick's hip as they are laughing. He feels thin and confident again and realizes how long it has been since a woman touched him and he didn't feel accused of something.

She isn't young, not much younger that he is, anyway. Maybe thirty-six. A good thirty-six. A very nice warm lonely thirty-six. Just divorced.

You'd be surprised, she says, you'd be surprised what people put up with when they think they're in love. She gives him a knowing, slightly drunken look and asks, Are you in love, Fred?

I guess you could say I am, he says. I'm married.

Mm-hmm, she says, the colour in her cheeks rising along with the sweet red liquid she draws through two straws. That's not what I asked.

Well, I am, he says, twisting his hands one into the other on his lap. In love, that is.

Then what is it?

What is what?

What is IT? Why're you here? Thinking about it.

Maybe because Frederick can't answer the question, he goes home with her that first night. While they are making love, he watches a high-speed slide show of his wife, as if she keeps shooting past him in a train while he waits at a crossroads. He can almost hear the steady peal of the railroad bell as he moves rhythmically on top of Beth.

Afterwards, he goes into the bathroom and stares into the mirror, half expecting to have changed. Behind him, he sees a pile of soiled bed sheets stuffed carelessly into a plastic laundry basket. He feels arbitrary, like an interchangeable part, and more than a little bit foolish.

Still, his weight hasn't bothered him all night, and it is only later, when he is pulling on his corduroys, that he feels the doubling up of flesh around his middle and remembers.

Walking home, it is as though he has shed half his history
– the half that has been distilled through Julia's eyes.
Distilled, interpreted, applauded or found wanting. He has
shed, for he doesn't know how long, a kind of sadness that
comes from knowing too much about himself or someone
else. And he suddenly sees himself as he might an interesting
but slightly frightening stranger.

Hoping that the air will blow Beth's smell off him, he
decides to tell Julia that he had dinner with a client. But
Julia doesn't ask, and when he switches on his bedside lamp
to undress by, she turns over in her sleep. In bed, he tries to
picture Beth's face, but it keeps disappearing after each split
second, making him wonder what kind of a man he is.

When Frederick goes out to meet his mistress – a term he
keeps bumping into and batting down – Julia waves
goodbye from the second storey window of their corner
brownstone, wishing him luck with yet another deal. They
have begun leaving the windows open – it is getting warm
– and one night as Julia waves goodbye she hears Frederick
curse. It is then that she begins to wonder if he is lying to
her.

She sits up that evening looking at photo albums – mute,
smiling, sun-burnt faces staring up at her. She is trying to
see if a difference in Frederick's expression from any one
page to the next might reveal just when things changed. But
she can't find many recent photographs and she gives up,
thinking, We mustn't like the look of one another any
more.

That Thursday, Frederick takes off his suit when he comes
home from work and puts on a fresh shirt and clean
undershorts. When he bends, a vein in his neck bulges,

making him appear suddenly virile. But in untying his shoe so quickly he has gotten the lace into a knot that with his thick mannish fingers he cannot get out. Julia stands in the hallway watching him undress, for the first time in months. It is all so obvious, she thinks. How stupid we both are.

Don't hold dinner for me, he says, without looking up.

I won't, she says, looking at the crown of his head bent over his task – pulling a fresh pair of beige socks up over his thick calves. You're losing your hair, you know, she says, after a pause.

Frederick stares at her for a moment. Thank you, he says, confused by what his wife notices and does not notice any more. I won't be late.

She waves from the window and when he turns the corner she pulls a lemon-coloured cardigan around her shoulders and follows him. Her low heels click. She curses, but she doesn't have time to go back and change. So she walks the whole way on the balls of her feet and after a few blocks her calves begin to burn.

She follows Frederick to a restaurant on the waterfront. Two sides are glass, to allow for a view of the bay. Julia sits on a bench with her back to the water. Frederick faces the head waiter, who looks down at his desk and then leads him to a table near the window.

He orders a drink and a boy in a black bow tie and white apron brings him something very tall. It looks like a double. He is nervous, Julia thinks. She wants to laugh, but cannot. Several minutes pass, fifteen, perhaps twenty, and Frederick is still alone. He flicks with his finger at the short tassels hanging from the tiny lampshade in the middle of the table. He leans this way and then that way, as through trying to look like he belongs to the party on either side of him. He puts his head in his hands for a moment, until he realizes how forlorn this looks.

Pathetic, Julia thinks.

He leans back, so that the front legs of his chair lift off the ground. He is conscious of being on his own. He and Beth don't go out in public very often. He thinks about leaving. But Frederick is too polite, even while cheating on his wife. He feels this about his own character, is disgustedly at home with himself. He feels as though his personality – his life, even – are comprised of bytes, which he knows by heart and just keeps repeating. He wishes he were another man. He pictures Julia at home and it all feels so funny, like they are going out of their way to do absurd things to one another. Things that once they would not have known how to do.

Julia pushes toward the edge of the bench, as if to go to him in a crisis, forgetting for a moment the circumstances. Maybe I am wrong, she thinks. I shouldn't have said that about his hair. I should never have said that. I should have asked him where he was going. I never even asked him. When she realizes that she cannot go to him, it dawns on her for the first time that she is spying on her husband.

Julia sees a woman standing at the waiter's desk. She winds her way towards Frederick's table, but he does not see her. People are getting up from another table, blocking her way. Julia smiles. This pale woman, standing patiently in the middle of a restaurant as if waiting for a light to change, could not be Frederick's lover. She is too nondescript to be anyone's lover. She is dressed in grey – a grey skirt and a short grey jacket – both too heavy for this time of year. Her white blouse has one of those billowing bows at the neck that Julia hates. There is something decidedly sturdy about her, and Julia feels sorry for her, imagining that she is hard-working, unmarried and childless.

But then Frederick stands and smiles and kisses her on the ear. His mouth lingers there. What is he saying? Julia's lips are shaping a question, then shaping her husband's name, repeating it. A certain thing has clicked into place and stopped, like the dials of a watch jamming.

So it's true, she thinks. Now what?

The woman is explaining something. She is moving her hands about, explaining why she is late, Julia supposes. She touches Frederick's cheek with her palm. She moves around the table to sit down, squeezing her bottom between two chair backs. When Frederick draws the grey jacket from her back, the woman pushes forward with her breasts, and Julia blanches at their fullness.

Frederick and Beth are chattering and occasionally touching. When they drink their wine, they make a toast. To what? Julia wonders. Does he say something poetic? Something vulgar? Something promising? When they eat, they do not pay close attention to their food, the way people who have not enough to say would do. And yet, Julia thinks, it isn't sex, and she cannot believe that it is love. There is sex, of course, there has to be. Good sex. It's these dull women that remind you of pencil lead that are full of all the surprises. But she cannot understand why the woman is not younger, or prettier. Frederick *is* handsome. She feels a stirring for him that shocks her. Frederick runs his hand through his hair, thinking, Julia knows, of losing it. She's filled with a surprising mix of pity and satisfaction for having made him self-conscious in front of his mistress.

Frederick is laughing. The two of them are. What the hell is so funny? Suddenly, Julia wants him home, laughing with her. Filling their house with loud, uncontrollable laughter. Sitting on the edge of their bed, loosening his tie and chuckling over something, anything at all. Julia begins to weep. The big picture windows and the coloured clothing inside and the small lamps with the tassels are swimming. Frederick is like a stranger she is dying to meet.

Frederick and Beth skip dessert and coffee and when Julia looks up, their table is empty. She pulls her sweater and her purse tighter to her chest as if to hide, thinking that they might go strolling on the waterfront. But they are only paying their bill.

Frederick lifts his wallet from the back pocket of his pants. The sight of him fishing with one arm behind him and his elbow cocked is as familiar to Julia as is the smell which he carries home with him each night. His own mix of sweat, deodorant, carbon monoxide, coffee, his work, the bar after work, other people with whom he's mingled. He sometimes takes a shower after work and Julia can hear from the kitchen the water running above her. She remembers the sound, like an actual memory of a person who has passed from her life. She remembers her husband – clean damp and flushed from the hot shower; steam gushing in billows from the opened bathroom door. She can see his towel knotted at his waist, the soft swirl of dark hair on his belly. She hears him padding through the hallway above her, contending with his own cache of miseries. What does he think while he is dressing? When he looks at her potions on the vanity and her clothes slung over the wicker chair back? What does he think when he looks in the mirror or while coming down the stairs to join her or when he catches the first aroma of dinner? She promises herself to ask. Frederick pays the bill and waves back the change the man offers him. He was always generous, she thinks.

They cross the main thoroughfare and head in the opposite direction to Frederick's and Julia's house. When Beth stops and bends to look into a lighted shop window,

Frederick checks his watch and Julia curses him. When Beth stands again, he is expansive with her, still laughing, talking, touching her arm with his hand sometimes, bending close to her to hear something she says. She points to another shop window and they both laugh. When Julia passes the same window she cannot imagine what the joke was.

They arrive at Beth's apartment building and Julia realizes that she has come as far as she can and that her reward for all this is having to watch her husband climb the stairs to another woman's bedroom. But when Beth takes out her keys, Frederick puts his hand over them and kisses her on the cheek, thinking what a coward he is.

Not tonight, is what he says.

He tells her it is late and that he has an early start and she accuses him of just not wanting to. Just say it, she begs him.

He bows his head and shakes it and she tries again, by putting her index finger under his chin and lifting it.

But he is thinking of his own unhappiness, still asking himself, Why am I here? She repeats his name, once seductively, and a second time, imploringly. He gives her only a sad stare and says in a voice she can barely hear, Just not tonight.

While climbing the stairs Beth thinks, He will leave me. She knows this, even before Frederick has admitted it to himself, certainly before he admits it to her. I have begun to make him feel dirty, she thinks, and he will leave me.

As Julia watches her husband walk away from the lighted, glass-doored foyer, she remembers the way they used to walk at night in years past in the spring. Ducking into cafés or movie houses or watching the ships dock on the waterfront. Some of the ships they knew – they each had favourites – and they would welcome them back like old friends. Standing at the edge of the dock pointing at ships and birds and funny strangers that caught their eyes. Walking home together.

Frederick stops and leans against the side of a building, his head touching the wall which has grown cool with the night. He looks at his watch again and even the unwelcome gratitude Julia felt disappears. He thinks he has enough time after all, she says to herself. But what he is thinking is that he cannot go home. I am a coward, he thinks, and I smell like lies. My wife will watch me or she will ignore me, and either way I couldn't stand it.

He walks on for three or four blocks before going into a bar. Julia is shaken. Though it is she who has trapped him, she feels it is the other way around. Because now she must either act or go home and await his return. She goes to the window of the bar. By standing on tip-toes she can see through the neon lettering to the inside. There are lanky young couples clustered around small circular tables. Old men with bulbous noses, who are either too fat or too thin, are sitting alone. There is a fight on the television. A middle-aged man with an open-necked shirt moves back and forth behind the bar. Julia sees her husband's profile, the same one she has seen all evening. He swallows, then fills his cheeks with air so that they puff, and slowly exhales. He buys a bottle of beer and puts his head in his hands, like earlier, only this time he leaves it there.

When Julia steps inside, Frederick lifts his head and turns in his swivel stool towards the unoiled door, expecting to see Beth. A shock wave – barely palpable – comes and goes. And then a sadness settles on him. It is the same sadness he felt lifting after that first night, only now he is comforted by its return. He looks at his wife and presses with his palm on the empty stool beside him.

Fireflies

Even before I noticed anything strange about my mother, I noticed Mr Schiller. He used to visit us on Jasper Street, that summer they were hardly ever apart. It's a summer I remember by its sounds. The bang of a glass on a table, followed by peals of helpless laughter. Flat palms slapping off the table like exclamation marks of mirth. Music. Sleepy stuff like you'd hear in a lounge, where you couldn't tell if the singer was a man or a woman. This, late at night and accompanied by a different kind of laughter. Softer, stratified, instead of all at once. As though the laughter itself were a conversation. An occasional stumble and then a small crash, usually accompanied by more giggling or, less often, by coos of concern.

What I noticed about Mr Schiller was his hands. They were large and fleshy and seemed to have no veins in them at all, and they always shook. When he lifted a cup of coffee or smoked a cigarette or poured bourbon into his tumbler. I put it down, at first, to the strange ways of adults. I figured maybe Mr Schiller was just nervous. Maybe he loved my mother and he wasn't sure if she loved him back. Or maybe Mr Schiller was scared of my dad coming home and finding him there and beating him up. I was a little scared of that myself sometimes, even though Mr Schiller was a big man. Or else it was one of those palsies, or it could even be that he was cold though, like I said, it was summer. It might have been any of these. But one morning I realized that Mr Schiller was a drunk, and that was why his hands shook.

I was sitting in the kitchen watching cartoons when he came to the house.

Johnny, he said.

Hi, I said, without looking at him.

Where's your mother?

Still in bed.

Still in bed, eh? Lazy bones. Heh-heh, he tried to laugh but it got caught in his throat.

He sat down beside me and his breath was toothpaste and liquor mixed. I thought of a boy in my class. He came from what my mother called a 'wrong family' and everybody knew his father drank. When he dropped Kevin at school in the mornings in their big old Buick you could smell it from feet away. Dizzying, stale, fermenting fumes mixed with something sterile. Mouthwash maybe. The same smell that was coming from Mr Schiller. A smell I'd never caught off my mother. And so I knew she wasn't really like him.

I started looking for more ways to separate them.

First of all, he was a man. And, as far as I knew, only men were drunks. I'd never seen a woman on the wall. The wall was Hanneman Street and it really was an old brick wall, stretching unbroken on one side of the road for three blocks. It was where they all congregated, or maybe they lived right there on the sidewalk. They didn't sit like normal people, that was the first thing you noticed about them. The way their backs were propped against the brick and their legs were splayed and their heads were lolling to one side.

Once my father and I were walking down Hanneman Street on our way to somewhere. He was holding my hand. He jerked his head towards the bottles lying empty on the ground or wedged half-full, high up between the men's legs.

Meths, Johnny, he said quietly. Lethal stuff. May as well be drinking lighter fluid.

I nodded solemnly, not understanding, but still noticing that there were no women drinking these meths. Which was a relief to me even then, even when things were still OK with us. I'd have worried about them, out there among the rough-looking men and the strange stains on the sidewalk that I imagined could only be blood.

You never saw women drunk on television either. Only men, stumbling around and slurring their words. I didn't know whether they were actors, or actors who were drunk, or whether they really hired people who were drunks, but they were men, that I could see. And while they all seemed to me to be exaggerations of Mr Schiller, they bore no resemblance whatsoever to my mother.

The reason things got bad was because of my father. The way he left and never told us where he'd gone or that it would be for good. So we sat there waiting. It reminded me of a movie I'd seen where two cops are waiting for this guy they've arrested to come out of the bathroom. He's taking for ever, but they just sit there like idiots until finally it dawns on them to check, and of course he's escaped out the window. The curtains are fluttering meaningfully. I remember the look on their faces – it was a comedy – dumbstruck and dopey. They started batting each other over the head with the sports section.

Dad did send us money, though, from all sorts of places. The postmarks were never the same and I used to clip them off the envelopes and save them, the way I knew kids saved stamps or postcards their parents sent them from holidays. I imagined he was on a holiday somewhere, or working maybe, and that when he came home he would be impressed and moved by the way I'd tracked his movements so precisely, like the FBI sticking pins in a map. I did this until my mother found them in my room and threw them away. She said more than once, *I can't believe it*, and she looked down at the little squares in the palm of her hand, like they were the shattered bits of some precious belonging.

At first it was just in the evenings. She'd put on her red dress and light a cigarette and sit waiting for Mr Schiller to arrive. Sometimes she made herself a drink and she would gently sling the ice around the glass, her legs crossed at the knees, her ankle swinging in circle-time with the ice. She looked a little like a movie star then, and I wished that he'd never arrive. That we could just sit in the living room the whole night, with my mother all dressed up and me beside her, like famous people just hanging around, acting unimportant in the way that only important people can.

You'll be OK, won't you, Johnny? she'd say. You don't mind me seeing Mr Schiller? He's a very nice man, you know.

I always nodded. Yes for being OK. No for not minding. Yes again for him being a nice man. I guessed she didn't feel she had much choice any more, and I was sorry for her more than anything, and ashamed of us both, for reasons I couldn't quite make out. But I could sense that something had gone wrong in our lives, and that an element of sadness had entered it, which we seemed incapable of counteracting.

When he arrived, she would fix them both a drink before they went out and while she was in the kitchen, Mr Schiller would try to talk baseball with me. I only liked the Red Sox, and was only interested in the fortunes of other teams as they affected mine in Boston. Otherwise, I didn't much care, and whatever it was about him, he wasn't someone I wanted to share the Red Sox with. So I nodded again, dumbly. Yes the Phillies were on some roll. No the Dodgers should never have traded Rodriguez. Yes the AL East was going to the dogs.

Finally, the two of them would go off to a restaurant or a bar and he would leave her back home some time after midnight. From my bedroom, I could hear my mother sitting up on her own for a while, the flick of her lighter, the way her shoes dropped to the floor when she lifted her feet to the coffee table, more ice in the glass. Sounds. But these I didn't mind, since they were my mother's.

It wasn't long, though, before Mr Schiller started coming in with her. And that's when the other sounds started. Because it was late at night, and because I couldn't see them, the images conjured by the noises they made grew frightening and grotesque. When that slow music played, I imagined the two of them dripping about the living room, as though made of some viscous liquid. Then I thought how thin my mother's swaying hips were, how thick his hands, and I pictured him flesh and her just bones. Tumblers crashing on the table became great wrecking balls smashing through the sides of glass skyscrapers. And the laughter. If it was loud, then my mother and Mr Schiller had grown huge and ugly, their features distorted, like drawings in the newspaper meant to make buffoons of people. And if it was soft and milky, then my mother was dissolving.

He never stayed the night. It's not that they weren't

sleeping together. They were. It's just that she wouldn't let him stay the night. Because of me. That was where my mother drew the line. I heard him pleading with her several times. Always variations on the same theme.

I'll be gone before daylight, he'd say.

Pfff, she'd say. Before daylight.

I promise.

You're incapable of making a promise.

But I just have.

Keeping one, I mean.

I beg your pardon!

You heard me, she'd say, not unkindly.

C'mon, he'd say, lower this time.

And then there would be silence, while he tried to woo her, wear her down, slide his hands up her dress or nuzzle her ear with his lips. He'd make headway, too, because I'd hear her giggle or sigh before saying, even more firmly than before, No.

Just this once. I wanna wake up with you.

This kind of thing made my mother laugh. Then come over in the morning when I'm still asleep, she'd say.

C'mon, he'd say. I promise not to squeak.

Then there'd be silence again. But this time, my mother would be rebuking him in whatever way she did. Maybe pushing his hands away or giving him a farewell peck on the cheek, or else kissing him in a passionate but firmly final way. After the quiet, their chairs would shuffle and he'd get his coat from the closet or the sofa or the floor and they'd exchange two or three rounds of goodbyes, a buzzing sound to their speech that was peculiar to the late at night.

The evenings began getting earlier and soon Mr Schiller was spending days with my mother, drinking. She seemed almost frantically happy during that period and would often kiss me if we passed in the hallway, saying, Johnny, I love you, you know how much I love you. Don't you? And once, stroking my cheek, she said, This won't last, baby, don't worry. And then it seemed she looked as confused as I did.

Though he was at our house more and more, Mr Schiller and I spoke less and less. Mostly I relayed messages from my mother. Some days, she would send him away when he arrived, or rather I would, on her instructions.

Johnny, she'd say, tell him not today. Tell him stop by tomorrow.

Then I wouldn't see her face until evening, but at least I knew that she might be home with me. She'd sit with me and watch TV. Baseball or sitcoms or whatever was on. She didn't seem to care. She'd just stare and if I looked at her or spoke to her, she'd perk up, her eyebrows raised in an unintended parody of someone paying attention.

But other nights, she'd call him wherever he was – she always seemed to know – and go to meet him. Those were the worst times. When she'd be sitting there with me and it wasn't enough.

One morning, when I was sure she would, she didn't send him away. Tell him I'll be out in a minute, she said.

She came out in her bathrobe, which she'd never done before, though I could tell that she had brushed her hair. She whispered a few words to Mr Schiller in the kitchen and then she said to me, Johnny, would you mind doing me a favour? Would you mind cutting the grass? No, on second thoughts, don't cut the grass. Never mind. Just go outside for a while, will you? It's such a nice day.

I went out and sat on the back step and watched them

through the gauze of the screen door. My mother's whole body was shivering, and she twitched, like somebody with a tic. She spoke to Mr Schiller and he got up from the table and poured something the colour of tobacco into a glass and held it out to her. Only she wouldn't take it. She nodded towards the table and Mr Schiller put the drink down.

My mother took a few deep breaths and then she picked up the tumbler. The way it shook in her hand, it was like she was rolling a cup of dice in a game of Parcheesi. Like any second she was going to turn it upside down and dump the dice out. But she drank it instead. I turned away and walked out into the yard, knowing he'd done something awful to her to make her just like him.

After my mother got dressed, the two of them sat out the back all day, sunning themselves and laughing and drinking bottles of beer they kept pulling from a plastic ice chest. When dusk came, they went out for a walk around the neighbourhood. The moon was bright and the air was thick and warm and fireflies were slipping across the black sky like shooting stars. I chased them and captured them in glass, clamping the lids shut on them. Imagining they were stars.

When Mr Schiller and my mother came back, she said, Johnny, did you see the moon?

Her eyes had a sheen to them that matched the thin film of sweat on his forehead.

How could I miss the *moon*? I said.

Well, no need to get smart, she said.

They went inside and their low voices reached me from an invisible place. The light from the kitchen sifted through the tight mesh of the screen door. Mixing with their words and all of it drizzling around me.

After a while, my mother called to me. Johnny, what're you doing out there?

Catching fireflies, I said.

Fireflies! Mr Schiller cried. Let's have a look.

And they came banging through the door, their glasses, the liquor, glinting in the moonlight, and the two of them teetering slightly and squinting hard at the jam jars I had lined along the stoop.

Mr Schiller rocked back on his heels, one hand dug in his pocket and the other holding the tumbler tight to his chest. My mother's arms were crossed, wrapped around the waist of her sundress, and she was looking from the jars to Mr Schiller to me and back again. They seemed to be waiting for me to say something. About flight patterns or mating habits or life spans.

Finally, Mr Schiller said, Well, Johnny, what do you propose to do with those? He jabbed in the direction of the stoop with the hand that held the glass.

Just watch them, I said. Then let them go.

Hmph, he grunted. Doesn't sound like much fun to me. When I was your age—

C'mon, my mother said softly. Leave him alone.

Mr Schiller looked at her and shrugged, and then turned back towards the kitchen door, weaving as he went. My mother, her arms still crossed at her waist, twisted softly where she stood, as though to music. Her head was bowed and cocked to one side, and her eyes followed the fireflies as they bounced off the glass, each light in its own ellipse.

One by one I unscrewed the lids of the jam jars and we watched the sparks spiral back into the sky, like a whirlpool in reverse. Each batch dispersing until it was no longer a recognizable cluster. It was perfectly silent, except for the sound of threaded glass and metal loosing from each other and every time I opened another jar, my mother's eyes lifted towards the sky, a glazed, almost sublime smile on her face.

When I'd emptied the last of them, we both stared up into the darkness. I could feel her breathing there beside me, and the resumed sway of her thin hips. I was afraid to look at her, that I might lose her if I did. But though I stayed as still as I could, she touched my arm, and without saying a word, went back inside the house.

A Life

Syracuse, New York. 1953. He's smiling a winning smile, draping a towel around his neck the way athletes do. Thick dark forearms and hair matted wet to his chest. A teardrop of sweat trickles down the paler expanse of his side. Shiny tank top, shiny trunks that stop short at mid-thigh, where a perfect curve of muscle graduates into a kneecap. More muscle burgeoning below the knee – he has bulbous calves – and then, black canvas hi-tops. Simple laces. No Velcro in those days, no Air Jordans, no money.

She rushes to where he's standing and he kisses her, brushing her soft cardigan with his damp bare arm. She doesn't mind, though. She loves him so much, she thinks she must be the luckiest woman in the world. (Forty years later in a huge house by the sea, her friend tells the woman's children: He was so handsome, your father. We all thought your mother was so lucky . . .) She thinks for what seems like the hundredth time that day exactly what she thought the day she met him: Now there is a man.

He loves her too, very much. Loves the startling white flash against her red lipstick when she smiles. Loves the way she always knows just the right thing to say. Loves the way everybody loves her. They are what you could call a perfect couple: young, smart, aching to begin their lives after school and the war and narrow escapes from soul-destroying little towns where the grass grows in spikes through the

43

railroad tracks. She is beautiful. He is beautiful. They have picnics on the beach and together turn a lovely shade of brown. You can see it in photographs, even black and whites. They match. He believes in things like challenges, hard work, personal pride and getting what you want out of life. She believes in family, in commitment, in giving to the people you love. She believes that once you start something, you damn well better finish it.

He takes a job down south coaching a basketball team at a large university. (He's given up playing the game himself, driving to cold gyms for a few dollars a night.) Seems like a funny life to her sometimes – the way she gets dressed up in the team colours and cheers her heart out at all those games. It doesn't mean anything, she thinks guiltily, this thing over which he cries and curses and kicks chairs around a gym. This thing reporters call him up about at night, quoting him the following morning like a deity or a scapegoat. It's not like saving people's lives or inventing better ways of organizing the world. See, when she was growing up, she kind of pictured herself marrying a doctor, or maybe an engineer. But when she met him, she forgot all that. He was the one, as funny as it seemed.

Babies come. They have lots of babies. She wants them, and back then, who argued? Somewhere between the third and the fourth baby, it happens. She supposes, looking back on it, that it was inevitable; that his disloyalty was as inevitable as her loyalty. Tragic flaws. She knew about tragic flaws from teaching high school English, which is what she did before they moved south and started having all those babies.

It happens one night, when Mr and Mrs H. from up the street arrive at the house. A neighbour couple they play bridge with. The men golf together and make friendly bets on football games. The women sit in their kitchens in the hot humid southern summers drinking iced tea and talking about children and husbands and:

Oh, your hair is super!

Oh, do you know where I got it done? The new place in town on Pine Street . . . next to the Big Bear . . . a girl named Darlene . . .

Write that down for me, will you? I've gotta get something done with this mess.

On this particular evening, he and she are sitting out on the back patio holding hands and looking at the stars when Mr and Mrs H. arrive.

Pleasant surprise, he says.

Not so pleasant, no, Mr H. says.

Oh? she says.

Yes. And in a hard-edged voice, Mr H. tells her, My wife has been . . . *seeing* your husband.

She gasps, thinking, How could he? She must've made it up.

He winces, thinking, Why oh why did she tell him? All she had to do was end it.

Mrs H. looks at the floor and finally Mr H. says, a little more sadly, Well, what are we going to do about it?

What they do is, they just carry on. It's not that easy dividing children and chairs and incomes and affections. And they're both trying so damn hard. His regret is enormous – not the reaction of a hardened recidivist – and for a time the tangle of thighs and napes of necks and gentle curves that used to tempt him repel him. He pours all of his attention into her, more than she can take, really, planning Christmas celebrations and a New Year's Eve out on the town and romantic getaways. Just him and her and the moon.

★

A few years pass, during which she hears only whispers of things, certainly nothing like Mr H.'s hit-her-over-the-head-with-the-truth stuff. Nothing substantial. What she does know is that his friends treat her with a rather sad affection, as if to say, you really do deserve better. And yet, there are so many good times, good years, good nights of love and laughing and warm rooms and solid unmistakable embraces. So many gold-tinted autumn days when she looks out her kitchen window and sees him cutting grass — chinos and a clean white undershirt and his wristwatch catching glints of sun. So many lucky, lucky moments just like those, when nothing could be any better than it already is.

He's doing well. He's going exactly where he wants to go. And he gets a better job. This time they move west. She thinks perhaps that things will change for good, that the bad times are behind them. Something about 'going west' portends a clean slate, anyway. Doesn't it? (When was it exactly that she started grasping at straws?)

Things are different in the new place. The accents are flatter and the mountains much higher. It rains more and the earth is sometimes red instead of brown. The people have more money but are less real. But then he and she have more money now, too. Everybody wants to be around them. He is, in his line of work, famous. His thighs still curve with suggestive strength. His laughter is still conta-gious, his presence still a source of momentum. No wonder women try a little harder when he's around.

He thrives on it all. Becoming more of what he is instead of less, as she had hoped. And yet, it is still she who walks arm in arm with him from the arena each night. It is she who shoulders his dejected head after every loss. She is the

one still dressing faithfully in the team col
what he takes so seriously means anything or

But one night they are playing bridge. And
table, his stockinged foot caresses the nylon-shea
of the woman opposite. The insides of their thighs and
their faces twitch. He overbids. The woman redoubles his
bid. There is a moment of awkward confusion.

She notices. Oh no, she thinks, he's doing it again. Don't
tell me. He's doing it again.

He's fired from his job. It isn't really his fault – too much
pressure to win with too little talent to work with. It's the
first time he's ever lost a job and he takes it badly. People
stop inviting them to parties. Women stop trying so hard.
Men stop asking his advice. The papers just forget about
him.

He takes a job with a friend selling expensive condos in
the Bahamas. He works from home, giving time-share
seminars and mailing brochures to wealthy clients. But he
isn't very good at it. There's a recession on and a gas crisis
and he looks so unconvincing standing next to an overhead
projector instead of kicking chairs and giving interviews.

One afternoon she watches him from behind. He's sitting
downstairs hunched over an old desk with unsteady legs –
one they've had for years – adding a column of numbers.
On the wall, framed photos of triumphant moments: the
Conference title, the N.I.T., the N.C.A.A. semi-final win.
Two sweating whey-faced boys with smiles too big for their
faces holding champagne bottles above his head. Twelve
men caught in the act of feeling deliriously good. By God,
she thinks, he was happy then.

She's behind him, putting her arms around his neck,
kissing his ear. He's easily distracted and he stands to

embrace her, then closes the den door. They make love on the floor, being careful not to bump the shaky desk. They make love as if making their dying wishes. All the thoughts of fulfilment tainted with pain and ending and fear of the unknown.

(Afterwards, as always, it seems as if everything might just be all right. What's all this crazy talk about, anyway?)

They lie on the floor, chests heaving, and stare at the ceiling. His skin is damp and leaves faint traces on her cotton dress. She runs her fingers up the back of his neck into the short grizzle of hair, the feel of which she loves because it has never changed. Above them, a muffled conversation between two of their children. Laughter. The scraping sound of a chair being pushed from a table and then the front door closing. Sounds that accuse him of something. Sounds that remind her of her whole life: here and there and up and down, but always with all of them and never wishing it to be any other way.

But it's over and she knows it. She finds herself a part-time job and awaits the inevitable, remembering how many times they've kissed. How many times they've argued and eaten ice cream and driven for long stretches and made love and walked and cried and protected and betrayed one another. Not that any of that matters now. What matters now is that he doesn't feel lucky any more. What matters now is the way all the parts of her life are just flowing away from one another, as if a large icebreaker has ridden right through their midst. And all she can see are bits of a whole, drifting around in the cold.

But she doesn't make scenes. Suddenly, she is the one who believes in personal pride. And he is the one living in a cheap apartment with bad carpets, still looking for a job doing what he wants to do. Living in sin with the woman whose ankle he's spent two years rubbing under various tables.

He remembers the day he told his daughter:

I'm not helping you. Any more.

(She was living with a guy down at college. A gay guy, as he later learned, but what did he know about that? All he knew was that wasn't the way they carried on when he was her age. So she worked in a café and took out loans to help pay for her classes. She was so far away. Broke. Studying and working and cursing him.

And now, of course, here he is, six years on, jumping on the bandwagon of sexual freedom. Not just living with the woman either, but doing everything else, too.

It is one of his regrets, that he did that to his daughter. That he was so hard on her for the sake of what? Principle?)

Finally, he gets another job. A decent one. L.A., of all places. So he's back kicking chairs and doing interviews and feeling lucky again. He's still good at what he does, just lost a little faith is all. Now, he's thirty years older than the guys he's coaching. They're almost all black now and he's had to learn how to talk to them in this new culturally sensitive way. They're making three times the money he is and he has to remember to be culturally sensitive towards them.

Another regret: that he wasn't born later. Earning millions to do what he once did for the love of the game. His regrets are few, but they fester.

Three thousand miles away, she sits in the huge house by the sea. So handsome, her friend is saying. She nods, as if to say, Ah well, so much for him. Raises a glass to her lips and says instead, But he was a man, he was really a man.

Diamonds

Eddie steps out onto the small back porch and lets the screen door bang behind him. A hundred yards ahead he can see the baseball diamond, the high fenced backstop that hugged his son like a catcher's mitt each time he took his turn at bat. The sun is so strong it makes the green grass look gold. Or maybe it's just dried out, he thinks. There's no rain in this part of Pennsylvania in the summer, unless you're talking thunderstorms that sound as if the earth is cracking in two. But rain, just ordinary cool, silver-slanting rain. No.

He wipes the perspiration from his forehead, ignores the damp under his arms and lights a cigarette. The smoke rakes down his dry throat. He sits in one of the two cane rocking chairs and stares at the gold-green field, thinking he can hear the rising roar of the crowd as his son sends another ball over the far fence. Good man, Jackie! he thinks. Or does he say it? He isn't sure. Eddie doesn't even realize that he's smiling.

Maman's gone to do the shopping, won't be back for at least an hour. Maman. That's what Jackie called her when he was young, and now Jackie's children call her that, though they all live far away and seem stiff and bored and shy whenever they visit. When they do come, they play baseball on the diamond or Red Rover in the yard, each side holding hands in a line, facing one another like eighteenth-century armies. In the evenings, they wear a path up to Freezie's, where the big white plastic ice-cream cone spirals towards the sky, as if trying to twirl itself right into heaven. Come to think of it, there really isn't much else for the kids to do. Visit the neighbours maybe, but they just say the same dumb things they said to them last year. Like, Ophf! Look how big *you've* gotten! It's hardly worth travelling so many miles just to hear those words. Even I know that, Eddie thinks.

Eddie comes from Tamaqua, fifteen miles away, where his family, like every other family in that scrubland, lived in a shed. His grandparents were Irish immigrants who were happy because they weren't starving to death. Eddie is happy, too, but not because of that. He's just happy. When he looks back on his life, he just sees pictures: births and college graduations and marriages and baseballs soaring triumphantly out of sight. A stationwagon full of children who wouldn't be there but for him. The small concrete front porch in the evenings, heat waning, playing cards. A glass of whiskey, the colour of tobacco. His first day in the mines. His last day. Maman. The way she used to ice a cake – smooth back and forth strokes like a symphony conductor. Not altogether bad mile markers for anybody's life. Eddie's got nothing to be ashamed of.

He'd remind you of a faded beauty if you could see him. Lost his hair, his muscle tone, his ruddiness. Lost his insides, even. His lungs finally turned to cinder and he coughed them all up while Maman and Jackie looked on, horrified.

But there was something about Eddie, even when he was breathing his own ashes, something that told you there was life there once. Great robust hilarity and this room-for-everyone kind of love. He was one of those charmingly irreverent men that pious women fall for. There was something about him that even when there was nothing left, told you there'd once been so much more.

After Eddie died there in the hospital in Pottsville, just a final rasp like a goodbye, Maman hardened.

In fact, everything became harder but she survived it all. From chopping wood to the family's almost forgetting about her. (It wasn't really their fault, though. They were living good lives far away and Linfield was the kind of place you had to remind yourself to come back to.) Her hands began to shine, bare, red and bulbous-knuckled, as if she'd been in a fist fight. Her skin grew transparent, with thin blue and red lines through it, like primary and secondary roads. She took in sewing to supplement her social security. She fixed her own windows, shovelled snow off her icy steps and one year, to the neighbours' horror, patched leaks on her own roof, her faded housecoat fluttering dangerously about her feet. But it was as if Eddie was there, instructing her, giving her a foot up, lifting the hem of her housecoat, bracing her heel so she wouldn't slip. She didn't laugh any more, though. There was only so much he could do.

She barely survived the loss of her leg. She didn't lose it to an axe or to a fall, but to a surgeon's instrument. Gangrene, they said, the lower half needs to come off. So suddenly Maman was sitting in a wheelchair forgetting her own name. Since she went into the nursing home the house just sits. None of the grandkids are arguing over who's going to get it when she dies. No strangers are enquiring about it. Folks aren't exactly flocking to Linfield, where even the sun is unhappy, ashamed of itself for having to highlight all that decay.

But before that, before things got that bad, they used to visit her at the old house. The grandkids and her daughter-in-law. (Her son comes separately. Maman doesn't understand this business of divorce. Sweet Jesus, she thinks, I'm glad Eddie isn't here to see this.) She brings them once a year or so in summer. But one by one they drop off, until only three of the kids come and then two, then one and finally, just the daughter-in-law, who takes her for a roast beef lunch in Pottsville.

But no wonder they never visit. They feel sorry for her. They love her, even. But do you know where she takes them when they come to her? She takes them to the new high school. Of all places to go on their summer vacation. But it's the town's premier tourist attraction. The principal, Mr Patterson, squires them all around because they're Jackie's family and Jackie's a little bit famous now. He's one of those who got out and made good. Jackie never hung outside the movie house smoking Marlboro after Marlboro, cussing and whistling at girls. He never got black-lunged and short-sighted from the mines. And Jackie'll never sit, retired and scared, watching the young people and saying things like, You wouldn't know the place, and the kids, they don't wanna go to school, they don't wanna go to the mines, they don't wanna go anywhere. They're all on drugs, robbing houses, fighting. S'not the same at all, for goodness sakes.

No, Jackie got out. And if his mother wants to show her grandkids the new high school, why Mr Patterson is proud to oblige.

Other times, she takes them to see her friend Nelly, who married a man one week before he went off to war and the very next week he was killed. Nelly never married again. Never even courted. Just sits all day in her dark little house talking about him to herself or to anyone who'll listen.

(Nelly's half-blind, so she doesn't even notice that the lights are out and the shades are down and it's two in the afternoon.) Maman thinks it's almost religious, Nelly's devotion. But the grandkids, they think it's a waste. What does she think? When she gets up to heaven, she's gonna get some purple heart like he did? Some special seat at the table for having been sad all her life? They can't wait to leave Nelly's. But when they get out into the sun again, they feel sick, as if they've just stepped off a ride they were too young to have been allowed to go on.

She takes them to Eddie's grave, too. See, Maman doesn't drive, so any time anybody with a car comes and says, What would you like to do, she says, Go see Eddie. So they go see Eddie, put flowers on his grave and say prayers, and their mother gives them little secretive looks that mean, just a few more minutes, you're being such good kids. And they're just so sleepy, from closed-up schools and dark, sour-smelling houses and graveyards.

The whole family feels sleepy every time they visit Maman. They loved Eddie's stories, the smell of his whiskey breath, and the way he used to tease Maman. His huge belly laugh that they tried to imitate, when he was out of earshot. It kept them awake. But Maman on her own was like – well, it was like if somebody said, I'll give you the bad news first, and he did, but then he went away and you never got the good news. So all you felt was sad and incomplete.

The grandkids have kids, who think they might have heard of Maman and Eddie. They heard something about money once. Eighteen thousand, they'd heard their daddy saying. Eighteen thousand, you're kiddin me! Inside the sofa cushions? I don't believe it!

They couldn't imagine eighteen thousand of anything, let alone dollars. They knew what a sofa was, though, and it had something to do with sewing and hidden money and this woman named Maman.

(No, dummy, her sofa cushions.

Maybe it was pirates.

There's no pirates any more, stupid.

Well, somebody sawed her leg off.

Yeah! Who did it, then?

Maybe it was for the money in the sofa.

Oh God, you guys don't know anything, do you?

OK, then, tell us.

OK. What happened was she sewed this money into her sofa cushions because, because, that's where she kept it.

But where'd she get all the money?

She sewed for it, stupid, don't you listen?

Nobody sews for money!

Where d'ya think your shirt came from?

Mommy got it in J.C. Penney's.

Somebody had to sew it first, though.

Un-unh.

Un-huh.)

They heard the belly laugh, too – the one that bursts out, like when they come up after holding their breath under water for too long. The laugh that turns into a cough and echoes down their carpeted hallways, bounces off the walls of their bedrooms. The laugh that finally fades, until they just wonder carelessly what that odd age-old sound is that keeps at them like ringing in their ears.

(It's like a scary story I read. It was called 'The Telltale Heart'.

Where'd you get that?

I got it off Dad's shelf.

You're not supposed to –
In the book, this guy keeps hearing this heartbeat in his basement.
Stop it!
Why're you scared?
I am not!
It's not that, anyway.
Then what is it?
It's just Dad doing that dumb laugh again.)

Finally, they figured out that the laugh and the sofa cushions and the woman with one leg all had something to do with each other. And just like that, they filed them away with all the other grotesque lore they'd heard and decided had nothing to do with them.

In the nursing home, Maman forgets things. But she also has the pleasure of remembering far, far back. Everybody expects her to be somewhere else. *She's somewhere else*, she hears them whisper. So she goes. Back to the porch. Without needing a driver even.

Eddie is in the mines, but he'll be home soon, sooty and sweat-streaked. Jackie comes home from school just in time to change before his father arrives. He eats peanut-butter sandwiches washed down with milk while he waits for Eddie to clean himself up, and then the two of them go to the baseball diamond. She watches them, curving along the semi-circle of brush and gardens towards the gold patch. Arcing towards the pot of gold, she thinks, now there's a nice idea. The clean, gold-green field, spanning out from home base like a scallop shell someone had once brought her from the seashore. She loves the order of it – the dusted brown corners and the white bases shaped like cushions that you had to tag before somebody tagged you. Jackie explained it all to her once and she understood.

To the left there's just the path up to Freezie's. Her house is on the end of a row of houses, so that it neither belongs to the air and the yard nor to the linked arms of other houses. Like the end person in a game of Red Rover.

To the right, the Swensens' porch is empty. She's glad. She doesn't feel like talking to anybody just now. She likes just rocking on the cane chair, watching Eddie and Jackie and the spring unfolding, the gold light kind of curling around them like God's arms.

Thwack! Jackie hits the ball. It glides, for what seems like days, just inches above the ground. Magic! she sighs. Doesn't even realize she's smiling. Crk-crk, goes the cane chair. The ball skitters between two basemen before an outfielder scoops it into his glove. Jackie slides into second and then pops up again, hands on the knees of his starched grey uniform. He's leading off, she says knowingly. Eddie is behind the backstop, fingers hooked like claws into the metal mesh, shouting, Good man, Jackie! Good hit! Jackie and Eddie and Maman in a line, belonging to each other. The crk-crk of the chair and the thwack of the bat and the soft sound of Eddie breathing cinders.

Death of a Salesman's Wife

First of all, she didn't really die, not in any corporeal sense.
But, believe me, the colour did drain from her face and
when she lay alone in bed at night, she was still and straight
like a corpse. Never languidly unfurling after love, never
clutching in the aftermath of a nightmare. Just still and
straight and dead.

It was around 1974 when it all fell to pieces. The world
went funny and we started doing things we'd never done
before. Like my brother Henry. He had to get up at six a.m.
every other morning to wait in a line of cars at the gas
station. Waiting for gas. It seemed like a violation of our
civil rights. Burt Reynolds posed naked for *Cosmopolitan*
and then there was the President. Every night we watched
him and his henchmen on TV. Hearings, they were called,
and back then people actually listened. But I'm not talking
about any of those crises. They were only subplots, red
herrings. The real drama was unfolding behind a bedroom
door, where two protagonists grappled discreetly with their
fate.

I didn't exactly hear it coming. There was nothing so
obvious as a screech of tyres or a slap-reddened cheek. In
the end, all the end amounted to was that nocturnal
cartoon-like tip-toe towards the front door and that shame-
faced hope that none of the floorboards would creak.

I was eleven at the time. We had just moved into the green

house. Sounds idyllic, but it's not what you'd think. It wasn't glass on the outside or even green. It wasn't heady with sun-trapped balm. Nothing not native to the Midwest grew there. Not bougainvillea, nor even hibiscus. It was a place of decay, in fact. But I call it the green house because the whole inside was carpeted in this vomity green colour you couldn't get away from. Like split pea soup, only without the warmth. It was a sign that things were going to get ugly.

My father was a salesman. I won't tell you of what. That would imbue him with a heart-rending pathos he doesn't deserve. My mother worked part time in a convenience store. I don't mind telling you that. She deserves all the pathos she can inspire. But my father's line was becoming obsolete, and one night at the 7–11, Mother was robbed at gunpoint. As I said, it was a time of transition. Of recession even. Each Sunday, they saw their *real wages* shrink to a shorter and shorter column in the newspaper's bar graph. I suppose it was like watching their dreams inch closer to subsistence level.

When they started out, you see, their world was aglow. Not even the romantic haze of a sepia print for them. Only colour would do. Only sunshine. Only the best for us, darling, it's you and me, we're gonna go places! They trusted in that. In the Midwest, you trust, perhaps because the earth is flatter there. You can see so far in every direction, you begin to think that nothing is being hidden from you.

I don't know what he hid from her, or she from him. Or the two of them from Henry and me, for that matter. All I knew was the silence, which got so still you were afraid to break it, like you'd hate to break the glassy-smooth surface of a pool. And I knew the sounds. Of disappointment:

You're staying over another night? But why? Of exaspera-
tion: I'm doing my damnedest, but you're not helping! Of
the gentle click of the bedroom door, and the glassy-
smooth, slipped-into silence that followed, which for some
reason never sounded quite right.

(Their sins, you understand, were those of omission, so
that rather than hurling objects or insults at one another
across the room, the two of them just petered out quietly,
like witnesses leaving the scene of an unfortunate accident.)

I remember, of course, the day they sat Henry and me
down in that green living room with the black and brown
furniture that didn't match. It was left over from when we'd
lived in gold rooms with beige trim and amber carpet.
Before anything got ugly. And I remember that it was
raining. Why does it always have to rain at funerals and
marital breakdowns?

You may have had an inkling, one or the other of them
said. I can't recall which. The way they were talking, one
would take up where the other had left off, as if they were
adding beads to a string that would eventually become the
truth.

You may have had an inkling, they said, that things
weren't exactly right between us.

See, it's just that —
Your father and I —
Your mother feels —
It might be best —
We still love you both —
Oh God yes! Of course we do —
Just because *we* can't —
It doesn't mean that we don't —
That you can't —

It has nothing to *do* with you!

They were adding beads, all right, but one or the other of them had forgot to tie up the end so all the beads were just sliding off again. It wasn't even beginning to look like the truth. And what in the world was an inkling? It sounded like it should mean the same as a wrinkle. Honey, could you iron those inklings out of my dress shirt? Or maybe they were those crinkly grey curls in your brain. In fact, maybe that's where my inkling would come from, if I ever got one. But I had no inkling. I hadn't even noticed that when she came into a room, he left, and vice versa, as if they were trapped on opposite sides of a revolving door.

I was five years younger than Henry and less likely to have noticed such details. But one day they figured I was old enough so they rewarded me with the truth. I was old enough to handle it. But what's old enough? My father's mother was seventy-five and she couldn't handle it. But then she wasn't modern like we were. She still trusted the President.

Maria, my father was saying.

Maria, honey, are you OK … ?

He had his hand on my hand and she had her hand on my thigh and I thought, Screw them, they're just touching me so they won't have to touch each other.

It must've been a week later, or maybe two, when I got up in the morning and he wasn't there. Wasn't there in the way of someone who will never be there again, not in the way of someone who's just nipped over to Wichita for a few days to refill some orders. I thought I'd heard a noise in the middle of the night. Some sort of creaking or snapping shut or shuffling that lasted longer and was more complicated than someone just visiting the bathroom. Maybe. Maybe I didn't.

Mom, I said, I think I had an inkling. Last night.

Get dressed, she said to the coffee percolator, which burped small billows of steam into her eyes. Get dressed or you'll be late.

I think it was another woman, though Henry and I still don't talk about it. He thinks it had something to do with him. Of course he does. He's a man. Men think everything that happens is because of or in spite of or in honour of them.

In a way, it doesn't matter why. Love just failed, that's all, just got smaller and smaller like puddles drying in the driveway after rain. Possibly my father looked at the ground on his way to work one day, saw his disappearing reflection in the oily water and thought: This isn't the only person I ever have to be.

And who were we to say, Oh yes. Oh yes it is. Just hold it right there, you. Right there in your driveway, in your pitch black bedroom, in your little green house that you hate. Don't you dare go anywhere!

We couldn't say that. All we could do was stand in the doorway waving goodbye, thinking it's time to get the damn floorboards fixed because we don't want to hear that sound again. But we couldn't help hearing it, again and again and again, lying there in our beds as still and as straight as corpses. Without really having died.

They Just Don't Work

Maevis is dead years. Frank only just dead. Nobody knows about Matt, still, after all this time.

It's dawn. Everything is pink and yellow at this hour, and cool to the touch. You can't yet see the sun, but you can feel it coming, its corona haloing the shingled roofs. Down the flat wide streets, bread vans and paper boys and a garbage truck banging, a man in streaked khakis hanging one-handed off its back. By ten o'clock the streets and the beaches and the promenades will be live as anthills. Crawling masses coating the surfaces of the town, as though it were a sweet thing.

Rita is sad, but not shocked. Time passes. People die. If we're lucky, we make peace with our children before we go. Or before they do. This is what she's thinking. She's mourning, but not in the way she's mourned contemporaries who've died suddenly. Futures lopped off. Wide stippled vistas gone blight-black. Not in the way she mourned Matt either, feeling her son slowly sucked away from her, as if he'd been caught up in a mob and carried off, his eyes wide with fear as he receded, her outstretched hands clawing the air between them. Frank's death is different. She doesn't feel cheated out of him. Her father was old, and he suffered in the end, just as Maevis had, so that death was a clenched fist opening to release him, rather than the crude snatching of a possession.

Rita opens the cyclone gate and walks along the side of the house. Criss-crossing its entire lower length is white wooden latticework that has always reminded her inexplicably of candy. She passes the faded orange shuffleboard court, its two tired isosceles triangles facing off. She remembers the terracotta and black discs scuffling across the cement on summer evenings, though shuffleboard, with its monotony and its limited demands, was a game at which no one ever persevered. It seemed to her, even as a child, a thing that belonged to an earlier, more patient era.

She opens the flimsy padlock and steps down into the dank half-underground cellar which spreads like a stain under Maevis's and Frank's house. In her quilted shoulder-bag is a roll of black refuse sacks, a turkey sandwich, a thermos of iced tea and a plastic tub of coleslaw she got yesterday at the Wynn Dixie. She has a scarf on her head and a man's Oxford with the sleeves rolled up, an old pair of jeans and white deck shoes. She looks like a newlywed from the fifties, heading for a picnic.

Rita is an only child. But there's not even really anything of hers down here. The dank sprawl beneath her own house contains the debris of her life and her children's lives and even a few things of Bobby's which she didn't bother to discard after the divorce. Matt's letters are there. He used to write every week and then, just like that, nothing. But that's the way those things happened, of course.

So it's just Maevis and Frank here, hovering in every corner and behind every pillar. Rita fingers old magazines and cushions, record albums and rolled diplomas. And every time she picks something up, her parents seem to scurry out from underneath. Like living things beneath a lifted rock.

There are cartons and cartons of books. Sydney Sheldon

novels, Taylor Caldwell, Ian Fleming. Maevis was a great reader before her eyes went. She'd lie on her bed in the afternoon, when the air was winter-still and Frank was having his nap or playing solitaire in his own room, and read.

Then she couldn't any more. She had to strain to see the print and at first she used magnifying glasses but then she said she couldn't remember so what was the point? Every birthday and Christmas and Mother's Day, Rita presented her with a new pair of magnifying glasses, thinking she must've misplaced the last pair. She never mentioned that this was the umpteenth pair she'd given her mother and where in the world was she squirrelling them all away? But finally, after several sweet acceptances, Maevis said, I can't recall a damn thing, you know, I can't *retain* any more!

So, chastised, Rita herself had taken the books from their shelves in the closet and packed them in cartons down in the cellar. Why she didn't give them to the library or sell them to the second-hand shop, she couldn't say. She pushes them off to one corner now and stares at them, the bosomy women and gun-wielding men, all matte-eyed and staring back at her like orphans.

Alongside the far wall stretches Frank's tool bench. Small plastic boxes filled with nails, tacks, brads, plugs, pegs, rivets, screws of varying lengths. A microcosm of the man's meticulous nature and the order he'd succeeded in imposing upon his and Maevis's life. She touches them all in turn, the way she'd touched objects in play school, blindfolded, guessing at their nature. Cotton wool. Glass beads. Flower petals. Lessons in texture. She felt the same sensuousness and slight danger she feels now, plunging her hands into the points and flat heads and cold metal of her father's compartmentalized life.

What do you do with these? Certain things it just seems strange to throw away. Stoves and sofas, shoes, for some reason, and now nails. In wartime, she could've brought them to a sort of central depot and had them melted down. Young women and children and old people and husband-less wives standing around a massive flaming cauldron pitching in their offerings. Everybody puffed up with pride. Frank would've liked that, his tiny bits of metal transformed into fodder for the cause.

There is a large aerial photo of Cape May. In it, the sea is a deep purple colour – the same sea which had always appeared blue or green to her. Pin-pricks of clouds are casting shadows on the strange pink landmass; the blue-white strip of water she'd swum in, now the width of a thread. Aerial photos were like that, negatives too. They made you realize how limited your perspective was, how many other ways there were of seeing things. How much could actually be put over on you. Cape May to her was bleached dunes and concrete sidewalks and sandstone federal buildings. It was her mother's ridiculous white bathing cap, with the plastic flowers affixed. It was her father's one-piece swimsuit – striped tank top and belted shorts – embarrassing in its modesty. It was her own tow-headed self. Nothing pink or purple about it.

Cape May, where the three of them had frolicked in the waves, and much later the five of them, and then just four. Where she and Bobby had come for weekends in winter, eaten chowder at the Fisherman's Inn, drunk hot toddies and watched the surf from their hotel windows, half-dressed and happy. Where nothing sad had ever happened to her. She puts the photo to one side for keeping. She's going to hang it in her kitchen, magnet it to the fridge, though it may as well be Mars.

They Just Don't Work

There are rows of shoe boxes, full of letters, each one with a year written on its side in black magic marker. Maevis kept every letter Rita wrote, which Rita already knows because Maevis was proud of calling herself an archivist.

She finds the year when the trouble with Bobby started. Or rather when she became aware that there was trouble. Her language in these letters, couched in half-lies, makes her face burn. Bobby was away, *investigating a job down south*. Bobby was *having to spend more time on the road*. Bobby has taken an apartment *closer to the building site*. Bobby will be home soon. *It's only temporary*.

Why didn't she just tell them: Bobby is leaving me. Now it seems so silly – it was going to be for ever so what was a couple of weeks either way? But she'd wanted to tell them in person. So, on her annual summer visit to Maevis's and Frank's house, she did. There is a gap in the letters then, while they are all together, and when they resume, a hateful new honesty prevails. Yes, Bobby is still living with that woman, she writes. Yes, it appears to be final. Yes, I have a good lawyer.

Oh, that she could have lived in that gap – that dark silent tunnel of their togetherness – that place where, because it didn't happen on paper, it seems, it didn't happen at all. But it had happened. She'd sat on deck chairs and sofas and high kitchen stools for two stiflingly hot weeks, explaining. She remembers that time so clearly for its astonishment, its tears, its prevailing sense of failure, its strange sense of imbalance as Bobby's side of the guest bed went unslept in. His place beside her untaken, everywhere.

Mixed in with her own letters are shorter ones from Matt and Chris and Dana. Amusing episodes Rita'd forgotten:

Dear Gram and Grampa: Last night Matt left his sneakers next

*to the toilet and Chris got up in the middle of the night and pee-
peed in them!! Can you believe it? Isn't that funny! We miss you,
Love Dana.*

Then, strangely, as Bobby begins to withdraw from their
lives, news of him is on the increase. (Comparatively, Rita's
workaday presence goes unremarked.) The children write
of him taking them to dinner or to a movie. Ordinary
purchases he made for them, banal advice, small favours, all
suddenly newsworthy. In a twisted attempt at sophistication, they defended not only him, but the times they were
living in.

She and Bobby divorced, like most of the couples they
knew. One day they're all drinking gin on somebody's
patio and – bang – the next day everybody's scurrying off in
all directions, as though a shot had been fired.

Rita never could understand how things got so far out of
hand. Big deal – who cared who was fucking who – it
wasn't about love. She couldn't speak for any of the others,
but she believed that when she and Bobby were old they'd
still be sitting across from each other at the breakfast table.
Kids grown and gone, time on their hands, two friends with
a reckless past.

Because it *was* reckless, it was bacchanalian, and while
Rita wasn't the worst of them, she'd been a willing enough
participant. She'd shared kisses in pantries and on quickie
trips to the liquor store during parties. There were other
men she was attracted to, a couple of crazy blurry nights.
One in particular when she remembers Tom what's-his-
name's big suntanned hands against the stark white of her
slacks, dancing in somebody's back yard – where had the
rest of the party gone – the two of them marvelling at how
her slacks were shining – glowing even – in the dark.
Remember how good his hands felt spreading over her hips

like that – sort of colonizing her – he was much bigger than Bobby and she was gripping his thick hard shoulders – there were sighs and lips on skin and the Tiki torches stuck around the lawn like scattered fires in some desolate wasteland and not a soul in sight, though they could hear laughter coming from the bowels of the house, as if it were haunted and they were young kids who'd squandered their pocket money on the privilege of being scared. Then something about a chaise longue and she's sitting astride him – they aren't doing it, they're too drunk, but they're grinding away like teenagers, her white slacks and Tom's chinos like kept vows chafing between them.

She couldn't say she hadn't enjoyed those little trysts, but that was all madness, of course. Nonsense. She didn't take it at all seriously. It was just what was happening at the time, everybody letting everybody else away with that little bit extra. Their kids were off getting killed in some bumfuck jungle and I mean, good God, wouldn't you expect them to go off their nuts now and again? But she loved Bobby, loved him. That was what was real.

Years and years and years ago, Rita's father had had a mistress. Maevis went home to her mother and said, I'm not staying with that man, that philanderer. And her mother – Rita's grandmother – paid a visit to the woman and informed her that she was not, repeat *not*, to ruin her daughter's marriage and that she was never, repeat *never*, to see Frank again. Which the woman didn't.

Maevis is dead. Frank is dead. The last people to whom Rita's divorce seemed a tragedy unique to her and worth lamenting. Even the children have grown blasé about it. The two of them that are left, anyway. When Matt went away to the jungle, she and Bobby were still together, waving goodbye arm in arm as he caught the bus for boot camp. How would Matt feel if he came back and didn't find them together? Matt would rail against it. He would consider it a personal affront, their divorce, and that would only be right.

Sitting there on a crate of Frank's record albums, next to the boxes, her palms face up on her lap, Rita has a slight headache, either from crying or from the dust. And she is so weary. It's only noon time, but her energy has waned. She no longer sees an end in sight. It reminds her of projects taken up as a child on rainy days. Enthusiastically at first, then wearily, wearily, as the rain grew less novel and she began to drag herself in and out of doorways, slump-shouldered, realizing that her popsicle stick and glue log cabin or her clothes-peg fort could not be so summarily executed. She just wanted the sun to come out again so that finite games with other children could be resumed.

Rita gets up and stretches. She looks around her, as if seeing things clearly for the first time – an aerial view of this chambered cavern. The midday sun has neither brightened nor heated the cellar. She walks from dark pocket to dark pocket. They are here, too, somewhere, those other letters. It was important to Maevis to keep records.

There must be mounds of them. Not to her, but to the President. Or rather to successive presidents. To the Department of Foreign Affairs. To the Veterans Administration. To the Department of State. To congressional people. She kept carbon paper copies, in which she punched holes and placed in three-ring binders.

She also kept in close touch with the relatives' pressure group in Washington, D.C. And each time a body was found or a vet turned up alive, Maevis kept the clipping from the newspaper and added it to the binder. Didn't matter to Maevis if he was on his knees and kissing American soil, or gaunt with a menacing goatee and a vacant look in his eyes, living with a tarty gook and saying he was never coming home. Maevis called them gooks, much to everybody's horror.

The thing was, when Maevis died, nobody took over the campaign. That was when Rita knew that none of them had believed for a long time. A shamed silence hung around the topic for days, like a heat so heavy it made movement unbearable. When they buried Maevis, they also buried Matt.

Thirteen June 1985. The day Maevis died. Nine years and fourteen days since anybody believed. Rita knew she didn't believe. A mother knows. It was the others who surprised her. Chris and Dana and even Bobby. It wasn't a sudden thing, her knowing that Matt was dead. She didn't sit bolt upright in her bed in the middle of a night at the exact moment Matt got caught in a crossfire or bayonetted through the stomach. It came to her gradually, in fits and starts, a complicated concept she grasped only slowly. It sunk in deeper, on birthdays, naturally. And on the anniversary of his departure. But, funnily enough, it was other wars that really did it. The increasingly clear footage of all those conflicts. They made Matt's life seem part of a grainy, irretrievable past, the ways in which he might've died almost quaintly obsolete.

Maevis didn't see it this way. To her it was a mystery. A mystery Matt was waiting for them to solve. Solving it was a compulsion for her. In fact, Frank often said it was therapy, though she herself would have called it a *formality*. I'm only doing what needs to be done, she'd say, to get him back here where he belongs. Maevis just knew that one day Matt would come home alive, as surely as Rita knew that he never would.

The letters are there in a large wooden chest of Frank's from his own wartime days. There are coiled extension cords on top of the binders; an electric heater the size of a two-by-four and a lamp with a neck like a spinal cord seen under skin or a bendy drinking straw; there are spider eggs and cobwebs and just general grit. There's a bag of light bulbs with a tag attached.

On the tag it says: *These light bulbs are fine, they just don't work.*

This is written in Maevis's hand.

And, in fact, they are fine. In the slim clear strips between the opaque glass and the threaded metal, filaments are visible. All the glass is intact, though the tops are burned grey with use. Rita unscrews one of the hot bare bulbs dangling from the ceiling, using the cuff of her shirt as a mitten. She screws in and tests each bulb in turn, but nothing happens. Maevis was right. She'd saved them anyway. Written out the tag at her little kitchen desk under the lamp with the pull cord, then carried the bulbs carefully down to the cellar for safekeeping because, after all, they were fine. They just didn't work.

That'd be Maevis, thinking very seriously to herself as she descended the lino-covered indoor stairwell to the cellar that you just don't use things up and then throw them away. No way. Not things, not people. We're all more than just the sum of our functions. She could almost hear Maevis saying it to Frank, when he came upon her in the kitchen and said, Good Lord, woman, where're you going with those? Then again, maybe Maevis was just off her rocker. Stockpiling for the next world war or the nuclear winter, though what use burnt-out bulbs would be to her then, well, even Rita didn't know.

She's dead now, Maevis. Frank too. And Matt, surely

he's dead. He's gotta be. Absolutely no point in thinking otherwise. I mean, if he comes, he comes, but he's not going to come. That's the main thing. It was over twenty years ago. Matt'd be forty-five now, she probably wouldn't even recognize him. Where would they even start with each other? No point at all.

The sun has dropped low enough so that a thin blade of light bisects the cellar floor. Before long, it will be setting on the bay, as it always has. As a child, Rita would have loved just once to see the sun going down over the ocean, over its suck and swell. She knew it did in other places, but she didn't think she'd ever be big enough or rich enough to get to any of those places. She used to race on her bike over to the bay and watch the last minutes of so many days. The slightest crease line of light, a needle pulling red thread through a pale blue sky. And then she'd turn away sad in the blue-black evening and cycle home, always with the same sense of deflation that she never quite understood.

There is dust in Rita's lungs. She needs to get out and walk, out in the air, in the light, where there is movement. She needs to let all this go. It's time. Let Bobby go. Let Matt go. Let her parents go. She can't hold them any longer, they were never really hers to hold. She steps out onto the concrete, over the shuffleboard court, towards the cyclone gate. Blinking like a baby up into the sun. She's left the little door to the cellar ajar. There is nothing to steal.

Family Photos

Mother is maniacal when it comes to family photos. She hoards them, she sorts them, she places them in chronological order in brightly coloured three-ringed albums that reach back into the previous century. Each photo is dated, and in her careless, loopy script, she writes captions below them. She doesn't say so, but this is to keep us from forgetting.

Also, she doesn't try to protect us. From who we were, or are, or might've become. Potential unmet, possibilities never realized, allegiances long dead or shifted – all remain untouched in her books, for her books are a record of the way things were at any given time, and not to what we know in hindsight.

I begin at age six. A bunchy, red baseball jacket with the patches of his favourite teams sewn down each side. He holds the hand of his little brother, who is redder and rounder than he. They are riding on a big boat off the coast of North Carolina, facing into the spray like men, their hair bending in the breeze. Family, country, baseball. They fill his small life.

At eight, he is thin and straight as a lamppost. Ears that stick gawkishly out from his head. His grin is far too big for his face – it nearly eclipses all his other features. His skin is very clear, though, and his hair still short and shiny. If he fills out, the photos hint, he will be handsome.

Then, that awkward age, when he is neither child nor adult. When he hurtles towards manhood and is afraid. In a plain white shirt and old blue jeans, he steers a wheelbarrow filled with wet, brown, just-raked leaves and glances over his shoulder at the camera. He looks, for the first time, as though he is not sure exactly what is expected of him.

There is a formal shot of Dickey from his senior prom. A very pretty date, with thick dark hair bobbed and held in place by a band. A large pink flower pinned to the strap of her dress. He stands honourably behind her, still with that same half-moon grin. His back is held perfectly straight, but his white dinner jacket hangs lifelessly from the sharp corners of his shoulders. He has not filled out.

A newspaper clipping. Some vaccination drive at the school we attended. Three of my brothers are pictured, their names printed below the photo, and one is getting drops of something in his eyes. Dickey, the caption says, stands off camera. And again, much later, at a brother's wedding. Dickey is standing to the side, but you can see from looking at the photo that his separateness is now the norm. No one is trying to pull him further into frame.

There aren't many pictures of just Dickey and me together, the two of us having been born so far apart. But in one, I am sitting atop his shoulders in the back yard. Though the ground is bare and hard behind us, Dickey is in his shirtsleeves, gripping my hands. My hair has fallen over my eyes, but I am smiling. I am not afraid of being up so high, unable to see.

As the photos become clearer and the colours brighter, our parents show signs of ageing. Skin sags from upper arms and drops from necks, as though their bones have grown slippery. We take less care when staging our shots. We are used to being a family now and sometimes even tired of it.

Pageboys and bobs have been replaced by long, straight, lifeless heads of hair. My sister poses shyly in a modest mini-skirt.

Dickey went to college. There was never any question of that. He was a straight-A student, a school record holder, tall and thin and scared and no doubt a virgin. Small imperfections in his skin came and went, leaving barely noticeable pockmarks. I turn the page and he is grown. Standing on the L-shaped path to our house. Bearded, roguish and strangely handsome. His companion is the same. His companion is now an attorney. Everyone Dickey knew from those days left him behind, as if he were a small boat rocking in a wake.

I don't remember any of that. I was too young. If it weren't for the photos, I'd think he'd never been happy, that he'd never cared, that he was always crazy. This is what I remember: scabies; a phone call in the middle of the night; boils; stench; bursts of laughter at odd times, cigarette after cigarette. My clean light adolescence sullied by his presence, which hung about the house like a pall, something having suddenly gone wrong.

Dickey left our home for good in the back of an ambulance. We woke one glistening, frosty morning to find him perched, naked and bird-like, on the next door neighbour's front lawn.

What's wrong with him? I said to my mother. What's he doing?

Sick, she said wearily, he's very sick.

Dickey was laughing and still naked when the three men came to take him away. One of them was very nice and he squeezed me on the shoulder and said, It'll be OK. Mother followed them in the car and I stayed home from school that day, lying on the sofa, watching TV, like I was sick too

That was fourteen years ago.

I'll tell you what I've done since then. I've denied him. When *I* was at that awkward age, I actually pretended I didn't know him. I have asked him, Dickey, how are you? and he has answered, Fine, and I have been relieved at having been allowed to play along. I have studied his disease, in a clinical way. For a brief time, it made me love him. When I've been drunk I've cried, but only when I've been drunk. I have, on occasion, just plain forgotten about him, and told people there are five of us.

And, finally, I started going to see him. Once I brought an envelope full of pictures, but he just stared at them, like it was somebody else, in somebody else's family. I realized, later, that all the photographs were old. That there had come a point at which we'd stopped including him, as though we didn't like the look of him any more. Now I bring money, or cigarettes.

He lives just out of town, down the road, down a steep driveway, in a halfway house hidden from the main thoroughfare. Funny old men and women live here. Those are Dickey's words. They're all crazy, he says, you know that, don't you? I am proud of him when he says this.

As always, I find him slumped in a chair. Some mustard-coloured, 1960s' style chair, with thin wooden armrests, wider at one end than the other. He is watching re-runs of *Get Smart*, a long lip of cigarette ash curving under its own weight. He wears an old nubby maroon sweater of my father's, the big navy P on the front – for Pennsylvania – curling at the edges. I kiss him and I hug him and then recoil. There is a putrid sweat smell to him and his face is dull and slack, though it is rioting with blackheads.

His hair is long. He doesn't cut it any more. Grey strands slither down his back. So funny to see him greying. And then suddenly I realize, he has lived through these years. His hair has grown, his lungs have blackened, his bodily functions have burbled along, independent of him, it seems.

His arms are rail-like and too long. Except for his slightly distended belly, he is still thin, but the musculature of his youth has receded and gone soft. His own bones have grown slippery. When he speaks, it is in bitter put-upon tones. Not that we say much. Sometimes we go for lunch which, between the ordering and the eating and the paying, mercifully involves other people and offers something to talk about.

We always go to the ice-creamery because he likes it. He does nothing now that is not a habit. He has succeeded in eliminating the element of surprise from his life. It forces me to remember the day I saw him walking through our downtown towards the ice-creamery for coffee. The sun was out. It was summer. And I turned a corner to avoid meeting him.

Hi, Dickey! The pimply girl behind the counter calls to him – almost flirtatious – and knows his order. This surprises me. I would've thought him too unsightly to be welcome anywhere. But then I am often surprised by humane acts appearing out of nowhere.

That's Suzanne, he says. She works here.

She likes you, I say, trying not to sound puzzled.

Dickey doesn't answer, just keeps click-clocking his tongue against the roof of his mouth. Suzanne brings our food and stands talking to us while we eat. She seems oblivious to the dressing that hangs in Dickey's beard, the fact that his hands are dirty, that his speech is unnaturally slack.

He ignores me and directs his questions at her. Where is the funny button she wore last week? What would happen if he pushed it? How many hamburgers did she eat today? Give us freebies, he tells her, we're all on welfare. Get outta here, Suzanne says, smiling. With the softest slap to his shoulder. Dickey laughs then the way he does – wheezy with air and spittle, and maybe not even at Suzanne.

I don't know if he thinks about women any more, in that way. He was always unintentionally charming. Suzanne has fallen for the remnants of that. I remember then the day when we still lived in town and Dickey brought a girl home for dinner. She was even more pitiful than he was and he sat on the other side of the room and didn't show any interest in her. Mom tried to engage the girl in conversation, but she just talked meekly about her 'hobbies' and looked at the floor. I wondered why he'd bothered. I wish that I could remember her name. If I could, I would ask about her, and Dickey and I would suddenly share a history.

Our visit ends abruptly, as always. I have to go now, he announces, and he gets up from the table without waiting for me. I pay and follow him to the car and we drive back to the house in silence. When we pull in the driveway, he gets out, still without saying anything. He's had enough of my company, and whatever it is I mean or don't mean to him.

In the house, orderlies buzz about. Crisp women who do not know that he hit home runs or took the best girl in school to the prom. The present is the only thing that matters to these people because everyone here has a past. I say to myself that Dickey is different. He is one of us, I say, meaning the family and the future and the outside world. What we loosely refer to as normality. But they know and I know, Dickey is no different.

I am not much different either, really, to other visitors. I prefer the cold radiator to the old upholstered chairs. I prefer to see my brother crouched in fearful isolation than to see him fraternizing happily with the other patients. And when I drive away, it is with relief and it is always too quickly. I hurry up the slope and my wheels make a spinning sound that I am sure everyone inside can hear and is laughing at. They all wheeze and cast knowing glances in Dickey's direction. They can laugh at these things, I think, they are so used to being insane.

There is a photograph I have in a desk drawer at home. It is of Dickey, aged ten. I know aged ten because Mother has written on the back: Dickey, 1960, Myrtle Beach. White hair, half-moon grin and over-sized ears. Red baseball cap pushed up and back, arms raised, making tiny muscles for the camera. Because the photo is in my drawer, there is now a square white space in an otherwise perfect album. But Mother has never mentioned it. She knows us too well.

You Used To Be My Mother

We hurry out through the slim front door, bound down steps onto cracked concrete and across the lawn, where a pot-bellied black planter sprouts only sticks. Central Avenue is near-deserted, splashed in unseasonable sunshine. We climb into the big white Buick and swing the long doors shut in a heavy arc. Mid-week with my mother.

Four blocks, five blocks, Larzi's on the corner, where we once bought ice-cream sandwiches and striped pixie sticks, which emptied coloured sugar down our throats. Then the new supermarket, the old grassed-in railway line. The Buick hiccoughs over. Eight blocks, Seventeenth Street. The aqua-coloured Shamrock boarding house with the Tara balcony. And then ...

That's the house, that one. Where we did our courting. See, my mother says, pointing first out in front of her and then in a steady backwards motion. That's where we had our dinner on Sunday afternoons.

Really, I say. Who lives there now?

I don't know. I think it's been sold again.

I try to imagine my mother and father courting over Sunday dinner. She must have worn a halter top and modest Bermuda shorts and he wore Chinos, a US Navy haircut and a pastel Oxford shirt. He played baseball for money before that meant much, and she was on the cover of a magazine before that paid much. There was a lot of adoration there.

We turn left towards the boardwalk and park beside the ramp. We will walk north, we decide without discussion. Her legs are shorter and her stride smaller than mine and I have to walk with stunted steps to keep pace with her. The sun slips behind a cloud and the ocean assumes a grey-green flatness. We both look towards the sky.

Shall we walk on the beach? I ask.

From the beach we cannot see the flatness of the ocean. We see instead walkers' legs making X-signs above us and beer cans spilling from brown bags under the boardwalk. The shells that crunch so easily under our feet remind us of raw eggs broken for breakfast.

Sometimes she steps to avoid them. Now and then she bends at the waist, hands still shoved in pockets, to inspect a periwinkle or the semi-circle of a clam shell. I imagine her doing this when I am not here, walking with her pocketful of winnings back to the old house, where she will dump them, sand and all, into an earthenware bowl.

Strange to think she was married for twenty-five years and yet not married for life. After that long, she must've presumed that Dad, if not exactly happy, was at least too tired to start over again.

Dickey was an omen. Poor Dickey, bearer of bad news, mirror reflecting shattered post-war dreams, laughing at those from whose loins he'd sprung. It wasn't his fault he was laughing, though. Poor skinny, crazy Dickey. As he grew older he began to slump, and with his sloping back and long arms and unkempt beard, he looked like a panel from the middle of an evolution chart. Dickey receded and we all grew up around him, like tall trees that shut the light out.

Now, he gets duller by the day. No more insane invectives that make the rest of us squirm. Now it's just one-word answers and no questions asked in return. Poor dirty Dickey, who even Mother has given up on curing. He is nearly forgotten, nearly forty, now settled into a 'life' that makes few demands on the rest of us. Mother aches for him every single day. She tells herself she brought forth a life that knows only sadness.

The tide is very high and creeping slowly towards us. The sun has reappeared and the earth blushes crimson in response. When we reach the damp wooden pillars which support the boardwalk overhead, we grasp them and swing outwards. We bump shoulders, laugh and brush the wet sand from our hands.

I feel silly talking boys with my mother, at my age and at hers. Guilty even, like I did back in the car, thinking about her life and what percentage of it now exists in the past tense. So when she asks me, Do you love him? first I say yes, but then I change my tone.

I do, I say, but we're different.

Well, she says, a good heart makes up for the lack of a lot of other things.

Not just now. Not just yet, I think.

Besides, she goes on, I picture a big buffet table. I've told you about it. And it's like people and you take a little bit –

You've *told* me about the buffet table, I say, and she is quiet then.

Peter had a daring streak, like his father, only without the luck. Seems like there were years when none of us could get a break. We began to joke, out of insecurity, that we were low achievers, that we drank too much, that we couldn't hold down jobs. The neighbours outdistanced us. Childhood friends embarrassed us with their tight-fitting lives.

But Peter struggled hardest. At thirty, he worked as a dishwasher, analyzing Reaganomics and the Big Bang in his off-time. He was recovering from a broken relationship with a blonde and a love affair with alcohol.

Mother remained a few steps behind, like someone carrying the train of a bride. Finally kicked Peter out when he almost burnt the house down while boiling an egg in the middle of the night. He saw her on the street a few days later. A bottle of vodka poked its head out between the two zipperheads of his square brown suitcase.

I remember you, he said, you used to be my mother.

It took her years to get over that.

Her face is growing very lined. She has made it up nicely, though I notice she is becoming careless the way old ladies do. There are small streaks of blusher that she hasn't blended in. My mother is growing old before my eyes and behind my back. She is beginning to look like my grandmother used to, years ago. This scares me. A couple in their sixties walk arm in arm above us on the boardwalk, their long legs moving in sync. I look quickly back towards the water, guilt rising up in me again like the tide.

After a safe interval, I ask, Have you met anyone nice lately?

No, she says, so naturally. I'm all right, though. When I think about it, tcht. She claps her hands gently to her head. We were so naive back then, she says. All virgins of course. No idea what marriage was about. Expecting perfection! Expecting everything. She is looking off into the distance, with an indulgent smile, getting a bit of a kick out of her shattered illusions. Your generation is wiser, she says. You don't buy into the fairytales that we did.

The wind is forcing its way through the holes in the line

of phone boxes on the boardwalk. It sounds like heavy metal played backwards. I laugh, and Mom thinks I am laughing at what she's said.

Max got married at twenty-four. He has three lovely daughters and a nine-to-five job having something to do with computers. Sometimes he has to work at weekends. His wife is a part-time legal secretary. Max and Lise love their children, and each other. He doesn't cheat on her. When they aren't working, they play with the kids on the jungle gym in their fenced-in back yard.

One night over dinner, when I was about fourteen, the family voted Max the most normal of us all. Of me they said, It's too soon to tell.

I know Lise reminds Mom of herself when she was first married. We all feel Lise is a little too delighted with her life and though we don't want her life, we envy the fact that she does.

What I want to ask is, does she miss making love? Is she jealous of her daughters the way all the latest books say she should be? What is the biggest compromise she has ever made? And what is her biggest regret? When was the last time she cried? Over what? I have seen her cry only once, when she slammed a finger in the door of the dishwasher. And once I heard her, over the phone, when she told me that her father had died.

We climb the steps back up to the boardwalk and the wind from the bay side of the island hits us. Mother's hair blows back from her face and her eyes smart and water. The warmth has seeped out of the sun and her cheeks are flushed from the quick change in temperature. She is still a beautiful woman. I want to tell her this.

C'mon, I'll buy you a hot dog, I say instead.

Rona is beautiful too. Small and petite like her mother. Disciplined and serious like her father. She is a painter in Washington. All her work is brooding. When we go to her exhibits we are impressed. Also, we feel sorry for her. She must feel very black inside to make the kind of pictures she does. I'm so proud of you, my mother tells her. And she is. But I see she is afraid, too. We are all afraid for Rona. She is very small and needs so much.

Mother is speaking between bites of her hot dog. I catch myself not listening but don't force myself to start. I am watching her mouth, though. The thin red coating of lipstick she cannot live without. A bit of mustard at the corner of her lip. I dab at it with my own napkin. I am watching her fingers, too. On her left ring finger she still wears her engagement ring, twisted and reset, so that it doesn't mean what it used to. Her nails are thick and white, unpainted today. And her hands. Wiry and strong and tanned. She has held us together with those hands. We scatter but, like shards of metal to a magnet, we come easily back to her and always to this very spot.

    ... So I've decided to sell it, my mother is saying.

    The house? (So this is why I was invited in the middle of the week.) I thought we agreed, I say, I thought we agreed we never would.

    She shakes her head no, and is still chewing the last bite of her hot dog, unmoved by what she is saying. If you want it, she says, you move down here and keep it.

    She is moving to the city, she explains, because the town is dying. Because she can't possibly collect any more sea shells. And because she's surrounded by old ghosts and even older people, like the man next door who calls her day and night because he thinks *they're* after him. He phones me from his closet, she says. Do I need that?

Of course we don't want the house. We want her to have the house. We want to feel that there is some vestige of our younger surer selves still ticking over, some constant waging war on our behalf. But Mother refuses to collaborate any longer. She has only enough time left for telling the truth.

We are sitting on high stools with red speckled covers, next to the hot dog stand. Our feet don't touch the ground. Her thin legs are crossed, one foot hooked into a metal rung, and she wears an over-sized down jacket. She brushes the sand from her coat and concentrates on sipping Coke through a straw. She looks young in that position, despite the bits of make-up I can see. Over her shoulder stretches the line of boutiques and video arcades, knick-knack shops and miniature golf courses. Nearly everything is closed for the season. Shelves emptied, metal shutters padlocked to the ground. Hand-written signs reading, We wish to thank all of our customers for a great season!

I look at my mother sitting high on her stool, like a school girl at a soda fountain.

Yes, I say, it's the best thing to do, the only thing really. When I think of it, it seems perfectly natural.

Hands
___

Little Stevie is in a box. His face the colour of red brick and his fingers long and webby. He looks shrunk, like he is in the middle of disappearing. Pete and Tess are sitting on stiff-backed chairs, staring at Stevie with their heads tilted. The rest of us take turns looking at him, never having seen anything so small so dead.

Uncle Jim lifts Stevie's hand and the limp fingers hang over his one warm fleshy finger. Like the seaweed with the knuckles you can pop. He stands there rubbing Stevie's skinny wrist between his thumb and forefinger. Jim's hip is slung to one side, just as if he was leaning up against a bar, but his eyes are glassy with tears. I think Jim is brave for touching him.

I ride in Jim's big Mercedes to the graveyard. We're burying Stevie in Greenville. Pete carries the coffin all by himself. I know exactly how the white wood feels, being held in Pete's hands.

After they put Stevie into the ground and people stop crying, we all go back to our house. Everybody drinks a lot. Uncle Jim takes me aside and asks me if I don't think Pete is a little … *funny*.

Funny how? I say.

But Jim just says, Anything you need, Mags, you come to me.

Mama and Tess are in the kitchen and I am sitting out on

the back step reading *The Chronicles of Narnia*. It's just after Tess's and Pete's wedding, way before they ever thought of Stevie. Tess cried on her honeymoon. This is what she's telling Mama. There were big plops of rain falling on Big Pine Key and Tess'd sat down on the cool tiles and matched them drop for drop.

But why were you crying? Mama asks her.

I don't know exactly. There we were sitting in this dark hot room doing nothing, saying nothing, supposed to be so happy. Seemed so damn pitiful, and … I don't know. I just cried.

Well, what did Pete do?

He didn't know what to do. He asked me why was I crying and when I couldn't give him a good answer, he kinda lost interest.

How very sweet of him, Mama says.

It wasn't like that, Tess says.

I am picturing Tess and Pete in their hot dark room with the rain falling. I am picturing Pete. He is handsome and always laughing and he has big white teeth and square brown hands. Once when Pete came over to pick Tess up before they were married, her and Mama were off up the street visiting Mrs Ganz. I got Pete a glass of iced tea but when I handed it to him, he put it down. He kissed me. His warm tongue was slipping around inside my mouth and his palms rolled over my hips, like we were dancing. Then all of the sudden, Pete stepped back and said, God … *damn!* and held the back of his hand up to his mouth. Goddamn, he said, *what are we doing?*

Pretty soon Tess and Mama came walking up the road. When Tess looked at Pete and said, Hi, doll, his eyes hopped off hers like broke billiard balls.

Before they take Stevie down to that cold little room in the basement of the hospital, the nurse in charge of Tess gives her a lock of Stevie's hair and tells her and Pete to take pictures of him in his tiny bed. So Pete brings in his brand new Nikon and stands over Stevie's stillborn body and starts snapping pictures. I say to Mama, I think that's creepy, and she tells me it is part of the *healing process*. But it's creepy, I say, and she just says, Ssshhh.

I am at the kitchen sink peeling potatoes when Pete comes up behind me. He puts his hands inside my sweatshirt and rubs them up and down my stomach, over my bra and then inside my bra. He pins me against the edge of the counter top and pushes up against my behind. Whispering Mags into my ear and moving faster and faster and his hands like creepers spreading over my skin. I make a fist around the potato peeler and arch my neck. This time he doesn't ask what we are doing.

A couple of weeks after Stevie is buried, Tess goes to one of those groups where everybody there has the same problem you do. All the women are very nice and when Tess tells them how she thinks she'll take the photos and the hair and dump them in the sea like ashes, or bury them beside her favourite rose bush, all the women say, Oh no, don't do that, hon. They all have little bits of hair tucked in soft linen handkerchiefs and photos of children born still.

So Tess saves the lock of hair just like the women tell her to. And she keeps the photos in her wallet. Sometimes she pulls them out to show people. Tess says, Wasn't he perfect, wasn't he just gonna be gorgeous? And everybody coos strangely, but nobody ever says anything like, *Show me*, or, *Lemme see that again*.

Pete is drinking a beer, leaning against our back shed. It is

July and he is clearing a patch of briars for Mama. He has little scratches all up his arms. I am looking out the kitchen window at him. He props his shovel up against the shed. His boots are caked with mud and he leaves them on the back step. The screen door bangs in smaller and smaller arcs.

One day I come home and Tess is on her knees in the garden, patting a lump of dirt around the roses she planted when she was twelve. She stands up and puts her hands on her hips and looks down at the ground like it's been a very bad dog. I think about Pete's hands crawling across my thighs. Me and Tess lying on her bed, listening to records. The times Tess lied to Mama for me. She stands there for a long time. Finally, she brushes the dirt off her knees and picks her wallet up off the ground.

Hiya, Tess.

Hi, Maggie, she says. I didn't see you there.

You staying for supper?

She shakes her head. No. Pete'll be home soon.

You OK? I say.

Yeah, she says. I guess it's just time to get on with things.

There are pieces of damp hair stuck to her forehead and neck. She gathers them all up and holds her hair on top of her head and looks over my shoulder. This wasn't the first time for Tess. It happened once before to her and Pete, but much earlier on. Tess had the miscarriage just like a period, and everybody treated it the same as one. Like, isn't it a shame, but hush.

In the winter Pete wears a heavy lumberjack shirt. He takes my ice-cold hands and puts them underneath the wool, against his bare chest. He squirms. He says, Damn, girl, you got you some mighty cold hands! He pulls me to him. He smells like earth and soap and woodsmoke. There is a soft thump in the pit of my stomach. Warm milk. Once I was at a birthday party. A blindfolded boy smashed open a pinata with a stick. Candy fell all over the floor. I'm like that. Split open, sweet things spilling from my insides.

I am sitting on the front stoop pushing a pebble around with a stick when Mama says to the next-door neighbour, I see the way they look at her. Men forty, fifty years old.

Scare the living daylights outta you, Mrs Honeyfield says. I know *all* about it.

Your Dolly was what, fifteen?

Sixteen. Still a baby herself.

Sixteen, Mama says, shaking her head.

Sixteen going on thirty.

Tcth-tcth. Mama clicks her tongue. One day you wake up and bang! she says, they got all the stuff you used to have.

They laugh.

I can feel them looking at me.

Finally Mrs Honeyfield says, Pretty girl all right.

Uncle Jim pulls in the drive. Mama and Mrs Honeyfield turn. They each keep one arm under their breasts and with their free hands they make little awnings over their eyes. There are moons of sweat under their arms. Uncle Jim's car glints in the sun. He has just come from his office. He has a charcoal grey suit on and he looks too big for our yard.

He tells me he'll send me to college if I want.

He leans back against his shiny car and says, I know things are hard. Don't think I don't. Money's tight, your mama's at you, seems like you gonna be fifteen for ever. But listen to me, Mags, 'fore you know it, you'll be outta here. And what're you gonna do? Where're you gonna go? The money's there for you, girl. You just say the word.

I wish you were my dad, I say.

Uncle Jim laughs and says, I'm like your dad. I'm gonna look after you.

I move some gravel around with my bare foot. I want to tell him about Pete. I want to tell him that, yesterday, Pete stood in the kitchen doorway, his hand like a claw cupped over his crotch. Instead I say, Well, I guess I'll think about it.

Once, Pete asks me if I like it.

You like it? 'Cause if you don't like it, I'll stop. Right here and now.

I have my back to his chest and his arms are wrapped around my stomach. I curl into him like he is a shell and I am a small fleshy thing that needs him to survive.

One night in April I come home from playing Kick the Can up the street in Elsie Ganz's front yard. Mama and Tess are sitting at the kitchen table. They're just shapes because it's almost dark out and they haven't switched the light on.

How come you're sitting in the dark? I say.

Tess says nothing, just pushes her knuckles against her teeth. Mama turns around and says, G'won upstairs, hon, Tess and me are just having a little talk.

Can I get some cookies?

Mama waves her hand OK towards the cupboard. I get a glass of iced tea and some Chips Ahoy. Halfway up the stairs I hear her say to Tess, A leopard doesn't change his spots.

Tell me something I *don't* know, Tess says.

OK, she says, OK. Listen to this. Forget about that *for*

ever crap. You got to start thinking about yourself for a change. Now're you with me?

Tess doesn't answer.

I sit on the top step, eating Chips Ahoy. Pete has a girlfriend in Greenville. She's due in June.

Tess and Pete never did make a baby.

Pete is gone now and Mama says it's for the best.

Tess is looking for a strange man to make her pregnant.

I'm not getting any younger, she says. What if I don't meet a man I like enough to have a baby with? Besides, I don't wanna be having babies when I'm thirty-five.

So you gonna do it with any old stranger they fix you up with at this clinic? What if he's a pig and you don't like him?

No-oh, Tess says. You do it in a dish. You don't even have to meet him so it doesn't matter whether you like him or not.

Well, that makes a helluva lotta sense, Mama says. Thank you for explaining that to me.

It's raining. It's only two o'clock, but it's so dark the air looks like ashes. Mama and Tess are shopping for material in Greenville. They wore their slickers and sloppy black galoshes and ran out to the car, cursing. There are pools of black water in the gravel, more of it running down the road. It's been raining for four days.

Pete lives in Greenville now. He drives a truck for the city. A big yellow one with orange pylons stacked on the back of it. I close my eyes and I am picturing Pete. I picture him and Tess at the graveside, propping one another up. Pete carrying the coffin under his arm like it was school books. I see Stevie's brick red face and his strange body that was more like an old man's, the way the breast-bone stuck out and the skin sagged from it. I'm thinking about Stevie's dark fingers, too, but not the way they were when Uncle Jim held them. Not cold and limp any more. They are part of a big pair of square hands now, flush with blood and heat and good for gripping. Holding a shovel or a steering-wheel or a woman's hips.

A House in the Country

They are sitting in a fifth-storey office, clutching hands, leaning forward on their stiff black chairs. On any other day, the fluorescent lighting from the plastic grids overhead and the hum of modems would have made them sleepy. But today is a day they've talked about for months.

The realtor who found them the house pushes the papers across the wide desk that divides them. He's done deals like this before. Usually the place is back on the market within a year, filled with half-finished jobs.

Yvette signs and hands the pen to Clark, her eyes lingering over her own signature. She loves signing her name. Unlike most women she knows, she actually loves her name. With its odd consonants bumping against each other, she thinks it looks exotic and worldly.

Well, it's final, she says, squeezing Clark's shoulders as he pushes the papers back across the desk.

Yeah. He reaches up to pat her hand. I can't wait to get started.

But not today.

No, he laughs, not today.

We need a celebration, she says, with new-found sophistication. What with signing her name and suddenly becoming the co-owner of a derelict farmhouse, Yvette feels intensely modern and yet laden with the responsibility of some age-old tradition. Pioneering, perhaps, she thinks.

A House in the Country

She takes a scrunchy satin band from her shoulder-bag and winds her long thick hair into it, then snatches at bits of it so that tendrils fall loose over her forehead. How about The Olive Garden?

Where else ... ? he smiles, clapping his palms against his thighs.

The Olive Garden is a restaurant and bar in the urban centre of renewed Wilmington. It lies just off of a pedestrianized avenue where infantile trees rise out of thin wire cages, desperate to look like they belong. If the neighbourhood holds, meaning if the right kind of people – people who respect trees – keep coming to the avenue, the roots of the trees will some day burst through the bricks and everyone will feel a mild sense of panic.

The Olive Garden is where Yvette and Clark first met, so naturally they hold all their celebrations there. But the place is beginning to fill with students, which they resent. Being shoved too quickly into the future like that. They sit in a high-back private booth, congratulating themselves, talking about how many of their friends dream of doing just what they are doing. Throwing off the shackles of the city, is the phrase Clark likes to use.

The shackles consist of two jobs, two apartments, two answering machines (which they both hate, but are dependent on), bills for things they haven't even worn or installed or switched on, office parties they grudgingly attend because it looks good and seasons that pass almost unremarked.

Like most people in Wilmington, Clark and Yvette have been to the country before, but they don't count those visits. They were years ago – family weekends in rambling farmhouses. If the sun shone there was always a stream nearby where the children would hunt for crayfish and

97

turtles. And if it rained, they chased one another through dank, panelled rooms, slipping on braided throw rugs, while the grown-ups sat around a shaky card table drinking beer and playing bridge or pinochle. The grown-ups were always strange during those weekends, though. Strangers full of rusty, collusive laughter.

Neither Clark nor Yvette has happy memories of those early visits, with their forced camaraderie and their shame-faced fumblings in damp cellars and disused lofts. They don't associate such fulsomeness with the country. They think of the country as a flat clear place, echoing with its own desertion. It has no parameters and no dead ends. It is strong enough to drive people away, whereas the city sucks everyone in, indiscriminately.

They rent a U-Haul to move their belongings. It is cold. Yvette tries to lean close to Clark across the void in the front part of their Toyota. When she is lonely or afraid she hates bucket seats. Though they've brought few possessions – choosing to store most of them in their parents' basements – they feel as though they are dragging a great weight behind them.

Our whole lives, Clark jokes. That's why it's so goddamn heavy.

Yvette laughs back, rather nervously, rather absentmindedly, and squeezes his thigh to reassure him.

Do you know, she says, while following with her eyes the rise and dip of telephone lines, that they've already replaced me at work?

Well … you did tell them to, he reminds her.

I know, I guess I just didn't think they'd find someone so quick.

Yvette worked for a firm which compiles and prints

in-house newspapers for large corporations. She hopes that after she gets settled she will take in work at home, like the women she's read about in magazines.

They've known you were leaving for a long time, honey. It wasn't as quick as all that.

She admits that this is true but, even so, she feels so suddenly forgotten about, rising and dipping without end, weighed down by whatever is in this U-Haul they're pulling.

To make herself feel lighter, she imagines things she will grow in her garden. Tomatoes perhaps, because Mom did and God knows she was no gardener. Herbs, of course. Yvette likes the way the tiny little green plants have such distinctive personalities. And potatoes maybe. They seem easy, taking root in thin air the way they do.

In the silence, Clark realizes that he is gripping the steering-wheel too hard. He relaxes and his mind drifts. He sees himself on one knee, in a pair of white overalls, the straps criss-crossing over his bare back (despite its being November). He has a hammer in one hand, a long nail in the other. One or two jutting like fangs from between his teeth. He is not sure exactly what he is doing. The image has no backdrop. Perhaps he is laying a floor. Perhaps he is building a bird-house. It doesn't matter.

The house, which they bought for next to nothing, is in New Jersey, inland, in what was formerly cranberry country. The big crop, they were told, which made them laugh, later, when they were alone. The cranberries they knew came in tin cans – dense rubbery cylinders they had never pictured growing anywhere.

There are two storeys, plus a cellar and an attic. The walls of the house are painted a pale aqua and shingled in large upside-down domes that remind Yvette of her own breasts when she bends over, braless, digging into her sock drawer.

The house has a wooden porch, which it wears like a low-slung belt around its square frame. A few rockers and two wicker settees sit on the front and back porches, to catch the morning and evening sun. Everything is in need of fresh paint.

Inside, there are two fireplaces standing back to back. The one in the living room has a huge raised hearth, on which Clark imagines he will sit until his back burns from the heat. The kitchen faces east so that they eat breakfast bathed in sun at a white tin table with wings that drop. Furniture left behind by the last inhabitants. The kitchen is large. In those days, they think, mothers cooked for big farm families and every meal was a jumble of heaped plates and steaming bowls and noise. They picture a family gathered around the oak table in the dining room, with its long slim benches and its two high-backed wooden arm chairs at either end. The dining room intimidates them with its expectations.

They don't think about children, but as the months go by and they notice small changes in their home – beauty marks that appear like crocuses in the spring – they talk often about their wedding day.

This summer, Yvette says. I bet the summers here are beautiful.

Clark shakes his head. Fall is better, he says. He is leaning back on the front step, chewing on a blade of long stiff grass.

Do you think so?

Mmm. Too hot in summer.

Bugs too, I guess, she says.

Loads, he says.

I can't wait for everyone to see the place, she says. I guess most of them will have to sleep at the Shilo.

The Shilo's not too bad.

Oh I know. I know. I was just thinking out loud.

Did you start your tomatoes? he asks.

Yeah, I can see some green vines coming up.

Good, I can't wait to taste the first one. He moves over next to her on the step.

Next fall? she says, after a pause.

Do I have to wait that long? For tomatoes?

No stupid! she says gently. The wedding ...

Next fall, he says, hiding her hands under his own.

They picture their wedding day. The living room filled with friends who now seem strangely crisp, loitering and laughing. Some of them reclining on the belt-buckle steps of the front porch, twirling wine glasses by their stems or studiously running index fingers along their rims. The off-white liquid sparkling in the sun. Their friends' children, who have begun appearing with a precision that reminds them of dummies in a shooting gallery, panting and running in purposeless circles in the back yard that never exactly ends. Yvette's and Clark's parents, who were never behind this whole house idea to begin with, saying things like, We've gotta hand it to you two, you knew what you were doing ... And later on, the older couples embracing in separate corners – kissing even – because pride makes them all feel young again.

Clark and Yvette don't have a phone, but they do have a small television. In the evenings, after spaghetti dinner or eggplant parmesan or stir-fried greens from the roadside market, they put their feet up and during commercial breaks they talk about the day. Yvette is tiling the kitchen walls, four-high rising from the old Formica counter.

I love the speckles, she says, the speckles in the counter. You just don't see that any more.

Or if you do, he says, they were just put there by somebody trying to look art deco.

Camp.

Camp. Yeah

I hate that.

Me too.

Miriam did that. And then she got those cupboards they call distressed. Paid a fortune for them, you know. She wanted it to look like a Swiss chalet.

A Swiss chalet in Wilmington, he laughs. You can buy any look you want.

Later, in bed, Clark tells Yvette about the gravel he must get for the driveway. Next week he'll go to Wilmington, where a friend of his will give him a good deal. She turns towards him, thinking not of him, but of the spring water they drink. Sometimes, little fuzzy strands like magnified amoebae appear in her glass. She knows they must be harmless, but still she feels as though she is drinking a science experiment.

Wondering what he'll haul the gravel in, Clark turns towards her in answer, and very gradually, very gently, as if they are afraid of breaking, they make love.

Their love-making is different out here. Beyond the bedroom wall, there are only other empty rooms. And outside, below the high window, only crickets and frogs and wind. No neighbours, no traffic, no orange-pink streetlights streaking in their windows. No sound of far-off glass breaking in a prelude to a crime. They should feel freer, but instead a strange shyness has crept into the bedroom with them. In fact, everything has grown quieter lately.

A House in the Country

Two months ago they noticed chirping sounds coming from the eaves. They were alarmed and wondered what to do. They did nothing and grew used to the sound. One day small tweets broke the silence and they felt the joy of parenthood. These moments of clasping and unclasping grow more pronounced between them. Now the birds have moved on and in the absence of any background noise, their periods of silence stand out.

Some evenings they drive to the Shilo Motel to drink beer, and though they are surrounded by people, the transience of the motel guests makes them feel lonelier. When they come home, Yvette is surprised by what she misses. At night time in her mother's house, the dishwasher was always clicked on, and from her bed she could hear it hum. A sort of period at the end of the day. She thinks often of her mother and father since moving to the house. Their almost passionless sharing of the day. The way they talk with their backs to one another which doesn't appear to bother them. Their marriage, to Yvette, seems a beaten path as dull as that which they have worn into the carpeted hallways of their home.

Yvette wonders sometimes if it's just mutual experiences that glue a man and a woman together. That the longer they live and the more of these 'experiences' they share, the less they depend on love as a reason for their togetherness.

(Ben and I have a history, she'd once heard her mother saying to a friend.)

Or, *is* it ever a matter of love? Isolated and equal to its origins, so that you never need this cocktail of shame and tears and marital dross to stitch you in?

On evenings like this, a little bit drunk from the beer, Yvette doesn't say much to Clark, certainly not about passion or her parents or her philosophy of love. Maybe tomorrow, she often thinks, but the next day it all sounds so maudlin. Anyway, at this hour of the night, Clark likes to read architectural magazines or the weekly newsletters he still gets from the bank where he used to work.

Tired? he asks softly, looking up from his reading. Her silence demands his attention and usually by saying, Tired? he means, Do you want to make love?

If she says No, that means, Yes I do. But if she says, Yes, that means, No I don't. On this particular evening, she says, Mm, I am tired. I'm going up. She bends to kiss him goodnight and leaves him under the lamp with his newsletters.

Upstairs, she hangs her clothes in front of the open window to air out the smoke – something her mother always did. They don't have closets anyway. They have wardrobes – extra pieces of furniture that house their work clothes and a few city suits that both of them feel silly for having packed.

When Clark knows that Yvette has gone to bed, he goes to the Dutch door and opens the top half of it. The air is slightly wet on his face. He can smell the beer and the smoke that the motel bar have left on him and wishes for a moment that he is back there. It seems like so long since he has sat in a bar with other men, just drinking and laughing and watching a football game on television. He can barely see the outline of Yvette's small garden, its few slim vines that have risen from the earth. He feels a funny sense of embarrassment for her. And then for them both. He starts to laugh softly and when he feels his movements convulsing into sobs, he backs away from the door and shuts it.

The morning he must drive to Wilmington for gravel, Clark is up early and Yvette stays in bed, curling and uncurling, unused to having so much space. Sounds from the kitchen race up the staircase: the bang of the toaster ejecting its contents; the scrape of Clark's knife across the hard bread; the deep sleepy voice of a woman giving news over the radio. Then, strains of 'Dream a Little Dream of Me' lift up like a refrain, and Yvette hums along, chasing sleep.

There are things she doesn't have to hear to know are happening. Clark's coffee sloshing dangerously up the side of his cup as his hard slicing motions rock the whole tin table. His absent-minded straining to see out into the black morning from his seat on the cheap stool gone rickety so fast. The kitchen itself, with its over-bright ceiling lights they plan to replace, its cookbooks not yet dog-eared, its corners where she cannot keep crumbs from collecting.

She hears his dishes clack into the deep chipped sink. He runs warm water over them from the tube-like tap. Clark does this every morning whether she is there or not. He assumes he is making her life easier and Yvette still can't figure out whether she finds this lazy gesture touching or infuriating. Through the slit in the drapes she watches the black sky grey. A door swings open and then shut. The time it takes to cross the yard, and another door opens and shuts. He revs the Toyota and rolls it slowly backward. When the last deep sound finally disappears, Yvette falls easily to sleep.

Losing Claire

Her parents didn't beat her. This story would be easier to tell if they had. But because she never came to school with bruises in impossible places, I don't know who to blame.

Claire would like to rewind her life, which is not an uncommon urge in the video age. If I could, I would rewind her life for her, and when I played it back, it would be filled with roses and pointed birthday hats and a shiny new bike lying on its side in her front yard. Fresh Oreo cookies for dipping into a sparkly-clean glass of milk while watching the *ABC After School Special*. A toilet that flushed. A house that didn't smell like wet dust. Parents who gave a shit.

The opening shot would go something like this. A girl who believes she's beautiful (she is) poses for a picture between her mother and father. They are all smiling. Her father is scanning the horizon, as if he might catch a glimpse of God and give a little wave of thanks or a thumbs-up sign. Her mother has what look like tears in her eyes – tears of joy – though they could be from the wind. Because the three of them are on a mountainside, out in front of a rented cabin, in the midst of a rustic family holiday. Tramping through the woods, spying deer, feeding rabbits, playing Hearts in front of the fire. Lots of belly-full contented sighs at bedtime. That kind of thing. And Claire, Claire is looking out over this vast valley scooping and swelling beneath her in the steely-hard October sun and feeling herself as big and as important as all the earth. She's loving all those little animals, all the different kinds of trees she can't name but her dad can; all the berries and toadstools and clouds and shadows of clouds, green grasses, blue mountain backs flat as slate, gulps of air. God's earth, she's thinking – for Claire goes to Sunday school in this life – it's not a bad place to be.

That's it, then, the outline for her life. Because once you have the outline for a comedy-drama, it's very hard to develop a believable tragedy out of it. I could leave you with that photograph and I bet you could throw anything at that girl and she would surface, sorrow streaming off her as easily as if she were coated with that special wax people put on their windshields.

Claire is twelve in my rewrite because that's the age at which we met. She smelled to me like green beans cooking in my mother's steamy kitchen, so it felt like I'd known her for ever. It felt right. Now, she is like a chunk of me that is slowly cracking off, and the gathering crowd inside my head is horrified.

Claire was born in the poor end of town, on the wrong side of the tracks and, no doubt, under a bad sign. A wayward father, alcoholic, amorous and elsewhere, an unstable mother, unfortunately ever-present. Four siblings who wouldn't speak to each other. And Claire. She worked her own way through college. Engineering degree, private school, *summa cum laude*, life of the party. That was Claire. The kind of a person who never needed a map and never got lost. Her life was logic grown out of chaos, like dawn burst from swirling black vapours.

After graduation, we took an apartment together. Claire

got a job in a bar, like a lot of our friends. But then she stopped getting out of bed in the morning. Slept all day. Never let me open the curtains. She was like a bat. Then one morning, she got up and said, I'm taking a trip. To Jamaica. I want to be with Rastafarians, smoke joints and worship Haile Selassie.

Fine, I said. Who's going to take over your rent?

Rent? she said. I'm talking about the one true religion.

She did hang out with Rastafarians and she did smoke joints but she didn't worship anyone, except a thug who beat her up. When I met her at the airport, she still had the jaundice-yellow spots of fading bruises. But at least she'd seen daylight. Her skin was tan and freckled and in her hair there were blonde streaks that fell like shafts of sun on polished pine. Maybe she'll be brave again, I thought, but she just went back to bed.

Three months later she said, I'm going to Canada. She found herself a little snowed-in shack in Saskatchewan and a Mountie who taught her to fish through holes in the ice and build fires without matches. When the thaw came, she returned to me and said, Ownership of material goods is the path to spiritual ruin. And then she went out to rent a video.

There were a few more Canadas – Morocco, Guatemala, Turkey, Goa. She became like a stitch threading its way in and out of my life. After Goa, she hardly spoke. But when she did, it was in torrents. One day she came home crying and said:

I was in the check-out line in the Safeway today there were so many people I had everything on the list I was OK but the cash register started going THRING-THRING a baby was screaming a clerk was smashing those big metal carts into each other I was shaking I couldn't swallow I had to squeeze out of line to leave the store only I forgot to put my basket down so the lady rang that bell that's like a siren the manager came after me so I dropped the groceries apples rolled out all over the floor people were staring at me and I ran out the door ...

Then she wrung her hands and said, And that's why we don't have anything for dinner.

Soon after that, she left me for the sea. When the city had begun to confuse her and she started needing less of everything.

I have to keep it simple, she said, for my own sanity.

That's OK, I said, that's good, in fact.

She moved up north, to a small town hemmed in by pines. To where the locals swap sadness like a secret handshake, as if happiness were akin to selling out. And to where the fog rolls in off the sea, like a grey carpet unfurling towards the mountains, the sea's heavy warm breath on the back of her neck.

We wrote letters to each other. Small normalities began to accrue in hers, like bits of punctuation she was learning. I started visiting her on weekends. She was nice again and laughed at all the right times. Small muscles took shape within the smooth pods of her burnished legs and arms. I felt as though I'd spotted an old friend coming down the street. But she was a watered-down version of the girl I'd known. It was as though she'd struck a compromise with God. In exchange for her sanity and a modicum of happiness, she had agreed to abandon what our parents used to call *amounting to something*. But at least she wasn't in bed all day with the curtains closed. And I loved her like I used to, in the way that reminded me of my mother's steamed-up kitchen.

She sent me madcap photos of herself. Claire in costume

on Hallowe'en holding an orange and black drink. Claire taking a bite out of six-month-old bread she forgot was in the oven. Claire shaving her head. Claire dancing on her roof in the rain. She held up her happiness for the camera the way some people hold up blue ribbons they've won.

But something was wrong.

Those small normalities slipped away again and her letters stopped making much sense. She was disappearing back down into that black hole of swirling sand and sea and wind. Claire was losing her mind.

It was hard for me to believe because I knew her when she was fearless. I knew the girl who'd written in her college year-book under *Immediate Goals*, 'Designing desalination systems in Africa'. I have a photograph of her on commencement day. A sunny afternoon in a Northern California town, her tasselled cap in mid-air, her fingers wrapped around the neck of a champagne bottle, Ray-Bans blacking out her eyes. If I didn't love her, I would've hated her because, in that moment, she threatened to do all the things in life that I would never be brave enough to do.

But then, suddenly, life had stopped. She just didn't know what to do. Some sort of malaise took hold, and her cherished goals began to quietly recede, like objects in the distance which had deceived her by appearing to be near.

By the time the accident happened, I hardly knew her at all. She was joyriding in a '64 Thunderbird and took a turn too fast. The G-forces swept her into the side of a mountain on one of those foggy days. She was three months in hospital, in traction, in the dark. In the darkness it all came clear to her. How she hadn't really given up her dreams and was being punished for that. How she was the product of neglect. She realized that all the laughter and all the faith of

those early years amounted to nothin
cards. That while I had foundations,
floor. And then she crashed throug
wouldn't be any doubt.

Since she's gotten out, she can't seem to
can't even decide what to wear, and when
supermarket, she gets lost in the frozen foods ....ed by
the sight of Tater Tots. They remind her of her childhood,
which suddenly she is aware of never having had.

Nobody comes to visit me, she says.

I visit when I can but, to be honest, what I want to do is
shake her, slap her face, as if it is all simply a matter of *coming
to*. She splintered but she has been fixed. Modern medicine
has knit her bones and sealed smooth her wounds. She is
without scars. It is only when I come closer that I can hear
her mind chattering, as though her skull has become a cold
place to be. I can see the strain of hanging on in her eyes, in
her crow's feet, even in her smile lines. Especially in her
smile lines, which are etched deep, like fossils of footprints
under frozen layers of earth. They are history lessons.
Somebody walked here, they say. Somebody smiled widely.

She still has her brilliant flashes. Crystalline moments that
glint like sun on champagne. But this blinding unan-
nounced joy of hers gets sucked back into blackness, and
just as she laughed at nothing, so does she cry. Watching
her fluctuate between exuberance and withdrawal has
become as terrifying and as riveting as watching the
magnified throb of an exposed heart.

The last time I stayed with her, I dreamt there was a giant
capstan in her yard and I had to keep turning it to reel her
tears back in. When I woke I lay there thinking, I would,
you know, I'd do it. I would rewind her whole life and all
the tears would go backwards and we would laugh again

had when we were kids in school. The way we had
when the teacher rewound the video tape and Hamlet
pulled the sword out of Polonius. All the blood raced back
inside and the open wound closed. We thought that was
funny.

Only Claire can't remember ever having laughed like
that. She insists she never felt so carefree. She says she was
like a tree in the city, imprisoned by wire, truncated and
choked by fumes, but admired for her stubborn explosions
of life. So now she is searching for a patch of innocence in
which to replant herself. A bare new sapling to grow up
straight and solid. It's a wild goose chase, though, and it
isn't funny any more. Claire is sliding down into an eddy. I
can see her hand reaching up to me, but the centrifugal
forces are so strong, they're tearing bits of her off. I am
losing Claire. And Claire is losing her mind.

Mythology

It was the week the black cat died that we almost made a go of it. We found her on the road, an untrafficked stretch of laneway in the country, not far from home. We were passing in the car and Charlie slowed down. I saw only the small white slippers of her paws, crossed daintily, and knew. Her blood had stained the tar and she appeared to have been dragged a short distance.

I thought we were safe here, I said to Charlie.

We have had four pets, Charlie and I. Three of them are dead. We aren't people whose animals will limp around our feet and trip us up. Old, feeble, and signs of something lasting.

Charlie got the spade from the shed and headed back down the road to where the cat was lying. The spade was propped against his shoulder and Charlie's chin hung towards his chest. Like he was heading off to some forlorn day of communal work.

Afterwards, we cried and stretched out on the sofa together. He seemed like a hero to me then, attending to the more painful and grotesque aspects of our lives, so that I wouldn't have to. Saying to me in the car: Don't look.

In the days that followed, we were kinder to one another. Attending to the smaller, most easily forgotten needs. Remembering things. We talked about the last cat we'd buried, the white one. They gave her a shot at the vet's and, rather than have her die on the strange cold table, we took her home and laid her on her favourite rug. Then we sat and watched the life just leave her.

With speed that surprised us, she stiffened into a C-shape, her body locked and hard as wood. I carried this curl of an animal up the back yard and placed her in the hole that Charlie'd dug. We'd only just moved in, away from the city, our minds full of plans. That was one of our first memories in the new house. But we needed better memories than that.

Rain, like needles, clacks against the window, and Charlie and I make love as best we can. With manners and a mindless attention to detail. In textbook terms, we *please* one another. We don't need inspiration or passion or even much interest, just that we be physically present, that we perform with precision. I lie there wondering if there is anything else in the world quite like sex, the way it drinks in insult and transforms it.

Around us in the room – a coat rack, a wicker chair, a stack of magazines layered in dust, wardrobes. This bed I've slept in, solid underneath me. The relentless innocence of our objects. I look at Charlie. Already, I see, he has acquired that sad beauty peculiar to people to whom we are lying.

This is where nostalgia starts. Because, of course, we haven't always been like this, and it's worth keeping that in mind. In the slack, grey periods that are coming at us faster and faster, the only place we can go for comfort is the past. Where had we been happy? When? What were we doing?

There is a lake in our town, and we're near the sea. There was a time we made an effort. Raking the sand for cockles or trawling in the shallows for mussels. We liked to

turn into the wind and get the full smell of th
is an image I've held onto. Charlie with his sle
up, his thick arms submerged, wrenching a shell
rock. Talking over his shoulder to me about wine
butter. Says he can taste it already. He kisses me before w
head up to the car. There is a tang of salt water on his lips,
and his unshaven face feels like a burn against my skin. We
look in our bags. We're all excited. Like kids with a booty
of Hallowe'en candy. It was silly, but that was how we
were. Anything we shared, we treasured.

If we can just get back there, we think, we'll be OK. But
whatever it is we're counting on is failing us. The bright
patches that used to stretch for months have become
pinpoints of light. And in between, there's just this dull
grey. What is disappearing is a sense of contrast. There are
no seasons, no peaks, no valleys, no midnight sun, nothing.

It isn't what we say that troubles us. We can clutter up
the air with words to keep other words out. There are
household chores to be divided, home improvements when
the weather cools. We hang out laundry and marvel at the
hot, hot sun which is melting the tar on the roads, the sense
of mirage everywhere. We make dates to meet friends and
talk about a break in November. A nice hotel, somewhere
south of here. As long as we can plan, we're safe. Once we
start looking only backwards, it'll be over.

A wind has risen in the valley, relentless and hounding. It
forces its way into our thoughts, so that we speak of cold
and warm air pockets, the long unbroken flight of condors,
hot-air balloons and hang-gliding. Anything at all. We're
out, having a drink. I look at Charlie's profile. If you've
ever seen an American nickel, the head's side, then you'll
know what I'm talking about. A set jaw. Strength. I look at

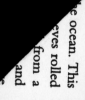

is dogged approach to each day,
the way the world really does
up angry too many mornings. I
ouching him. There is the thigh I
, the forearm, between his legs.
eling the residuals of love, like
ke.

es we brave it. Eat dinner by
ic to the beach. We spread our
wares on the blanket and focus on the sailboats stabbing the
horizon. Sundays, we go for long walks through the woods.
We do what is expected of us and await the desired effect.
But these acts are forms of cruelty. They only serve to
expose what's gone missing. If we can't love each other in
the moonlight, what chance have we got?

This morning we're drinking coffee outside. Charlie
looks at the sky and says to me, I think it's going to be OK.
He's talking about the weather – the day – but we both
catch his unintended meaning. He smiles, sheepishly, almost
pleased with himself. I can't help it. Charlie, I say, do you
remember Croyde? That beach that stretched for miles?

I remember that beach all right, he says.

I'm not talking about the beach.

Then what're you talking about?

Afterwards, when we went inside. Do you remember
that?

Should I? Charlie says, studying the sky again.

Well, I do. I wanted to make love before we went out.
Just for a change. You know what you did, you scoffed at
me, like I'd made a corny joke. And then when you saw
how angry I was, you tried to pacify me. You said we'd
make love when we got home that night, and I said, We'll
be drunk when we get home.

Charlie shakes his head and doesn't look sure I remember that, he says.

We weren't even married very long, Charlie. W supposed to be lovers, not people who found the embarrassing.

I wait to see what his response is.

I was reading in the paper there yesterday, he says finally, how people who don't know they're HIV positive live longer than people who get early treatment.

Really, I say.

I don't pursue it. I'm not interested in reminiscing. It's just that I want him to know. I want it entered in the record. That the turning points were times he doesn't even remember.

Our neighbour, Mrs Harrington, is lamenting the assault of weeds on her garden paths. She is passionate on the subject of their eradication. Charlie goes to our shed and roots out the sprayer. Mrs Harrington straps the cylinder gamely on her back, and in a hunched-over position, shoots poisonous liquid along the ground. She wears a mask and sunglasses, and looks like she is engaged in some sort of bizarre, not altogether legal activity. When she returns the sprayer to us, it is with an air of great triumph. Why, I wonder – when her house falls down around her, her husband drinks and goes missing, her children cry – does she spray the weeds?

Simple, Charlie says. Control.

I notice: our own garden let go, clothes flapping on the line for days, that I don't often look out the windows any more. The little grave with the stone to mark it. That one of the first things we shared in this house was death. In bed, we try not to touch. I keep quietly, stiffly to my side, and he to his. Making love has become an idea as strange to us as violence.

from one another, pulling
f taffy. The space between us
d yet still manages to contain
ccommodate things we never
Other people. White lies. Our
rate and closed, like two combat-
allway.

s at the tangibles. What's yours,
what s   u have come to love, what I have.
Which of us ca.   ar to give up what. It should feel
concrete, material. But it feels more unreal than real, as
though we are speaking in a foreign tongue in which
neither of us excels, or using profanity when we don't even
feel anger. We shake our heads as though we really can't
believe it.

It is this meek acceptance of our failure, our almost
benign embrace of it, that seems most profane. But that was
always our problem, that we were elderly before our time,
that the silence between us was a silence we hadn't earned.

There are boxes heaped in the spare room, waiting to be
filled. Charlie and I, we pretend not to see them. We
pretend we have not collaborated in this odious task of
gathering cardboard cartons from the supermarket. It
shames us to see our suffering reflected in such ordinary
acts. Every time I go to fill them, I stop.

All around, there are reminders. Roads it seems I'll never
drive without thinking of him. There are buildings, butcher
shops, wrought-iron gates, bends in the road, lay-bys in
which we stopped to view the exceptional days. There are
directions of wind, times of day, foods on the shelf, animals.
And water, always water.

There is the tall tree, the island, the jetty, the buoy, the rusty red and white boat, not moored where it was last year. The lake itself, his dream of living on it, the way I'd seen him slalom through it on one ski, cutting an arc of spray behind him like the plume of an old ink pen.

All these things belong to our mythology.

One evening, while mowing the lawn, Charlie discovers a plum tree in an overgrown corner of the yard.

Look, he says, *what we have*.

He is standing in the doorway, cradling plums in his arms, like some kind of windfall. A few of them drop and hit the floorboards in the hall, so ripe their skins split on impact.

Get a bowl, he says, and we'll pick them before they rot.

The sky is searing red on this particular evening. Charlie leaves the lawnmower humming low on the grass while we gather plums. More than we can eat. As we hoard them, greedily, I know that they will rot, most of them, in their bowls on the kitchen counter. But for a brief moment, we feel rich, in love again. We feel there is a chance. There is joy, fruit, a late summer sky. Tears smarting in my eyes.

I go back inside and dutifully wash plums, sorting out the bruised ones, and picking a few fleshy ones to eat. I sit down at the window and watch Charlie push the lawn-mower back and forth in the fading light. That old urge to touch him. That pinpoint of light. And then it's gone. I can see it. I see how tired and preoccupied he looks, and I know what he knows. That nothing is ours any more. We don't have anything.

Fourteenth Street

I am lying on the beach, though it's nearly six p.m. My face is to the ocean, so that two horizontal lines cut through my field of vision. First, I see the tans and whites of sand. Above that, a green, foaming sea stripe, and then, the vast, barely blue sky.

It is August, the time of year we always take our vacations. We are all here. The sun is dropping, the people thinning out until only we remain: dozing, reading, playing handball in the court Dad has drawn in the hard sand with his heel, burying one another in the softer sand, so that only our heads show. Bobbing, laughing, disembodied heads.

Stevie surfs. He isn't very good. Never will be. Surfing demands a bravado he doesn't possess. So he bends at the waist and skims along on a harmless lip of white water, close to shore. He read an article the week before about a surfer in Australia being eaten by a shark.

Dang, he said, guess the water's too cold for man-eaters here ...

Nobody bothered to answer. He seemed to be talking to himself, and, anyway, nobody knew the answer. After that, he wouldn't go out beyond his waist, and his timid surfing style grew even more so.

Catch any waves? I ask, when I see him coming.

Nah, he says, looking past me. Nothing worth catching out there tonight.

Over his shoulder I can
where a dozen boys tunnel
coloured boards adhering to t

Yeah, I say, I can see that.

How to explain the taste, the sm
those evenings. That feeling of un
only come from an absence of knov
Even the metal bins full of the day'   pot-
bellied fathers and the crying babies h   ssuring quality
about them. When I try to recapture it now, it is like
listening to a sterile re-mix of a beloved old recording. All
the white noise is gone and I am left with only gentrified
memories.

But back then. The air. The sea. The sun. All settling
together like welcome dust on this scene: a family shifting
in sync around the perimeter of an old green beach blanket.
Their games, the positioning of their chairs, even their
sparring, performed with the unconscious but affectionate
precision of life-long dance partners. I lie in the midst of
them, feeling the warm breeze dry salt into my skin. And
under me, the blanket, softened from years of August sun
and bodies damp with sea water.

I said the absence of knowledge, and yet there must have
been an inkling. Otherwise, every single detail of those days
– from the slap of a hand on a red rubber ball, to a sleeping
head hanging over the side of a chair, to the rangy gait of
my sister as I watch her walking toward the shoreline –
would not have seemed so inexplicably sad. Yet everything
was infused with sadness. At ten, I found the blank spaces in
my mother's crossword puzzle unsettling. Her pencil lying
idle on top of the newspaper. She quits, I thought. She

everything. How can I rely on her when she
ill in all the little white boxes in *The Philadelphia*

In one week, we will be home again. At home, I will cross
the golf course behind our house – such a perfect expanse
of green that it almost reassures me – alongside my brother
Tommy. We'll disappear into the coarse white sandpits that
dip between the greens and re-emerge holding hands, if no
one is looking. He is young enough to want to hold my
hand, old enough to worry that someone will see. In
twenty minutes we will reach the country club with its
three pools – baby, middle-sized and big people's – where,
in between swims, we will eat frozen Snicker bars and lick
the melting chocolate from our fingers. I'll miss the sound
of waves and the grit of sand between my teeth. I will think
an unformulated thought: that there is nothing like that
beach, that town, that house, that woman.

I was fifteen when she died. But wait, let me tell you about
her life first. Let me tell you about golden-fried chicken on
a platter being passed around the long table in her sun-
drenched kitchen. Knobs of butter melting into mounds of
mashed potatoes, forming rivulets that ran into the valleys of
our plates.

Let me tell you about happy hour, the snuck vodka in
the kitchen, the speed at which benign drunkenness
travelled through her thread-like veins, blurred her already
blurry mind.

Let me describe to you a woman in a polyester pantsuit,.
angry red bunions pushing through the sides of her cloth
shoes as she knelt next to her bed at night saying the rosary.
This is the same woman who made bathtub gin during

Prohibition and told pantheistic fortunes in her kitchen after dinner. This is the woman who used to bake three-layer chocolate cakes for our birthdays, but grew old eating beans from a can and spreading Cool Whip on a frozen pie from Sarah Lee. This is the woman who would've given me anything.

She lived in the beach house with her husband, my grandfather. Big airy place, but reeking of memories, even memories of acts performed elsewhere. So now, sitting in her living room, I catch glimpses of us out of the corner of my eye, like I would a cobweb or a fleck of lint caught on my lash. On days just like the one on which Stevie surfed and dodged sharks, she met us at the back door at about half past six, sucking up all of our happiness in the day. Some people are content just to witness other people's pleasure.

From her open kitchen door, which we had to pass to get upstairs to our half of the house, came the dinner smells. (My associations with her always come down to these: food; drink; scathing, off-the-cuff truths; the bleached white of my fingernails in summer and the ice that covered her back steps in winter.) But above all, the smell of dinner to a gnawing, child-earned hunger. I don't believe that people create scents like that any more. They certainly don't linger – beautifully slack-skinned, open-armed and humming – in the midst of them.

My grandfather wasted away too, of course. His plaintive whine rising up the steps so that finally my mother's visits consisted of nothing more than answering his calls. His masculinity – the virile accountant with the pencil moustache – reduced to a pathetic devotion to *Three's Company*. Some wisp of sexual desire remaining, teased out every evening by the sight of a dumb blonde in hot pants. His driver's licence revoked. His tiny lawn too big for him to mow. This is what a man becomes, I thought. And somehow it seemed worse than the disintegration of a woman.

We fight for the shower. One upstairs – inside – and one downstairs – outside. I like inside, where I don't feel so exposed. But everyone likes inside, so we fight, the tranquility of the evening shattered.

(I knew it would be sad. I knew somehow that it was right to be feeling sad about the things that made me happy: the bounce of sun off the water; the feel of my father's shoulders beneath me as we got out beyond the breakers, the white stains of dried salt on my feet at the end of the day.)

After my shower, I sit on the top porch, drying my hair. Mother pulls a comb through it, tickling my scalp. Beneath us, my grandmother runs the spigot, opens the oven door, calls to her husband, drops a utensil into her deep white sink. The sunlight bends and skirts down the alleyways, through the thin spaces between houses to bathe her speckled counter in brilliance. And I know, even as I hear her singing in the bright patch of her kitchen, that some day she is going to die.

Ice on the back steps in January. Fourteenth Street covered in snow drifts. Car's radiator frozen and forgotten in the garage. They don't drive any more. And at the bottom of the steps, hypothermic and hips splintered, she lies crumpled. Inside, his bony fingers drum an autistic rhythm on his knee, as he awaits her return from the grocery store. Since it is so cold, they will eat hearty stew from a can, heated in a saucepan on the stove she sometimes forgets to turn off and other times forgets to turn on.

Woman of my life, he thinks vaguely. His steady purposeful life that has progressed like the tap-tap-tap of his finger on his knee. This, despite the Depression, despite whatever year that was when they ceased sharing a bedroom, despite their only daughter's broken marriage, their grandchildren's strange addictions and choices and hairstyles. Despite all that, he and she have progressed through life together with a sometimes maddening and sometimes comforting momentum, like the alternating tick and tock of a clock.

And now, she is at the grocery store and the house is so quiet he thinks he can *hear* the air getting darker. It is almost five o'clock, in fact, very late for her to be out. He turns on the television but falls asleep before his show comes on. Heavy, dark cold outside and the house so still. No drink in front of him like usual at this hour, and no smell, even of canned stew, coming from the kitchen. So he just falls asleep.

On the beach today, child with my eyes surveying the long strand underneath the shade of her hand. She has batted a ball with some children she met. She has jumped over shin-high waves, squealing a strange and meaningless mantra my mother's mother taught to me and which I passed on to her. And now, she lies on her side on our blanket, bright blue nylon hooked taut over the point of a hipbone. Brown flanks stretched out unashamedly. Every now and then a glance over her shoulder to see what I am doing. I feel like telling her, I'll never die.

Love

Picture a silhouette behind a white wooden screen door. She wears a faded dress of floral print and a head scarf. Her eyes are blank, her arms locked tight under her breasts in what looks like resignation. Shortly, she'll hear the red rubber ball bounce against the shingles of the house, disrupting her dull reverie. She'll notice July clouds, low as steamrollers. Sweat in the creases of her skin. Her grey eyes as pregnant as the clouds.

There was a place for them. There were evenings of pure gold, the sun pooling on the floorboards. That light that could change from one mile to the next. Blackberries growing wild beyond the hedge, the juice bleeding into the lines of her palms. She used to slip her fingers between his lips and he'd give them back clean. His teeth turning purple with all that juice. So much colour, she said the world must've cracked wide open.

Autumn. The skip-rope rhythm of those days. A shin-high fog hanging over the fields, and a boy and a man wading through it. Talking with their heads bowed. Of something weighty, it always seemed. But no. The boy is young. It is likely only nonsense. What stars are or why nobody falls off a round earth.

Autumn, when the darkness began to fall faster. The air stiffened and the sky turned a dull white, and they knew before long there'd be hoarfrost. Cold snaps, then snow-bound. Everything stock-still. The dead of winter. Until one day, bulbs pushing through the black soil. Spring, the season of his birth. But that was the past. When there was comfort, even in the darkness.

A motel room. Off of I-95. Sheets a bit grey but the light was too so they hardly noticed. Outside their window, neon flashed like lightning. They heard conversations pass, low and indecipherable. Pretended for a while they were bandits and that those shoes scuffing in the parking lot belonged to officers of the law.

According to some record, it was the hottest summer. An old air conditioner hanging on the window pumped a strange cold breeze through the motel room. Dried the sweat on their skin, leaving a silty residue in its place. She curled closer to him in the dark and they laughed at all the imaginary crimes they'd committed.

Drinking beer in bed, that was what she'd said she wanted to do. Whatever pleased her. He used to smoke a lot in those days, and he held his cigarette to her lips. She took long drags that nearly made her dizzy, and rubbed her palm in a circle over his flat belly. Striped undershorts and a sleeveless undershirt. His taut skin as sticky as a surface that's been spilt on. She rolled the cold bottle across her cheeks to cool them. The comedian on TV telling jokes about the heat wave. Her head rose and fell atop his chest and the sheets grew tangled at the end of the bed.

The next day, speeding home, like being on a runway. The way the road was dead straight and the air quivered with the heat. She hung her feet out the window and he rested his palm on her bare summer thigh. She traced the veins in his hand, raised green rivulets of blood. Running thick up the inside of his arm, in the crook of his elbow, then higher, the jugular, his temple. The way the blood pumped through him.

She traced it back to that night in the motel room, between one of those perfect crimes. You always knew, somehow, just when it happened.

Her belly swelled. The air cramped with the cold. In December the pipes froze and burst. She thought of his warm veins in summer, fat and full.

There was a childhood, briefly. When the boy was learning to walk – bow-legged like they do – she'd let go of his hand and he would wobble to a gradual halt. A top losing momentum. Common things like that. His forehead pressed against the window pane, watching the rain flood the field, the creek climb its banks. A few deep blue summers. Dust rising along the steep blacktop up to the house. He used to stamp his feet, as though the dust were puddles, laughing at the way the earth billowed up about his knees, dirtied his white shoes. From small plastic bottles, he blew bubbles the colour of prisms. He loved the salamanders in the creek, the crayon-red of certain skies, the ground ridged deep and neat by tractors, their tyre tracks baked into the dirt. Overhead he saw jet streams, impossibly high. Then just soft puffs of smoke, then nothing.

One suppertime in April she went to call him. Shouted out over the back field, but he wasn't there. The panic came suddenly when she caught her husband's eye and it seemed to hit them at the same time. He ran out the back towards the creek. He was running through the trees, through the pale yellow twilight. Down the slope of the yard to where the ball had rolled, and to where the boy was lying, face down in the water. He could see a smooth skid of earth where he'd slipped in the wetness. Could see his head bleeding where he'd hit it on the sharp point of a rock. He dragged his son from the creek, tried to stem the flow of blood with the flat of his palm, pump his own breath into him. When she reached them she took the boy and shook him, as though he were asleep and dreaming of demons. Then she held him to her breast and sat beside her husband on the bank and they wept for what seemed like a lifetime.

There was a funeral, but all in miniature. Too little time to have cluttered up his life with mourners. The flesh, which had gaped and bled so generously, now neat and smooth; the boy blond and angelic and besuited. The beauty of it. The grotesquerie. Like a funeral in a doll's house.

Her head was on her husband's shoulder. He wore spats and a grey fedora. The grass was Easter green. The way their bodies just seemed to crumple as they watched the boy disappear into the ground. God, how they cried. She couldn't eat for weeks and her bones began to point at him like fingers.

They hardly spoke and, for a time, they couldn't bear to touch. Too much like mirrors, their worst failings writ large and looking back at them. Not smooth-skinned any more. Not brown, not veins or life-giving pulse. But turned inside out, all twisted and malignant. Whose fault was it? Those minutes when they looked away. When their backs were turned or their minds elsewhere and the boy dashed down the slope. The man had been in the carport planing wood. When he'd come up to wash his hands, he'd found her peeling something at the sink, staring blankly out the window, the emptiness of the yard not even registering.

Later, she wondered aloud if maybe he'd run faster and he said if she wasn't such a goddamned daydreamer. If you'd just kept an eye out, he said, and she came back at him flatly: You were there, you were right there. Did you ever tell him, he asked her, did you ever tell him how dangerous it was? If I told him once, I told him a thousand fucking times.

She used to hear him sobbing. Lean against the wall outside their bedroom door and close her eyes, listen to him like she might a tragic piece of music. His particular cadence. Quick hoarse intake of breath and then the long stuttering exhalations. The tears ran down her own face, until finally he'd stop and his breathing would slow and deepen and there was an emptiness and a horrible relief, as though a perverse kind of love had been made.

One day, she hears him singing. Quietly and to himself. A year, maybe more, and he's singing. She wonders whether she could ever hate him. But no. It goes on, she thinks, it has to. She remembers the way he used to sing to her in the car. Before the boy. Crate of beer in the back. Summer days given over to long drives. Fields without end, smooth flat roads moving through waves of gold. Pretend you're in the Panhandle, sister, and we're headed for the Rio Grande. Games they used to play like that. On the run from the law, bank robbers maybe, with the booty strapped to the chassis. The easy life waiting just south of the border. And then he'd sing some half-Spanishy song and snap his fingers bolero-style in the air.

Winter mornings, he leaves the house before the sun is fully up. Sometimes sits smoking in the car while the engine warms, staring at his own home as though he were a drifter with criminal intent. He puts his face up to the mirror, pulls his fingers down either side of it, slaps it gently, like a man just after shaving. Lines. A certain hoodedness to his eyes. He thinks of a deep untroubled sleep, of how slowly he knows this day will pass, how long the night ahead. A drink. He craves things in a new and unwholesome way.

Once, years ago, right there in front of where the car idles. The two of them sitting on the porch steps after supper. His back against the wooden pillar. Close your eyes, she tells him. She's feeding him ice cream from a spoon, catching the bit under his lip, like you would with a child. Four spoonfuls, five, and then she surprises him with a kiss. The odd coldness of their tongues. He opens his eyes and sees hers closed. Feels the weight of her against him. Few things better in the world.

They put the dishes away and drove down the hill towards town. Lights strung across the black sky. Like Christmas. Like Vegas even, that time they'd come at it from the west. Gasped. She had, anyway. Now, bouncing on the cheap upholstery. Drinking wine straight from the bottle. She touches him. His jaw with the back of her hand. Where the heavy shadow on his face becomes softer flesh. Suddenly, it seems like for ever. All that time in town and the long drive home again. No, they don't wait. He turns down a rutted lane, between the brambles, ignition off and they reach for each other in the dark. If he could freeze one frame of his life.

Sitting in front of that same house now. Wooden porch with the railings and the wicker love seat. Window boxes, bare vines twisting in a helix. The way the sun used to fall on summer evenings, when their bare feet were propped against the railing and over the radio all the biggest news came from elsewhere.

The paint began to peel and they scraped and sanded and repainted. Same house all these years. Eventually, it began to feel like patchwork – each repair – a little bit embarrassing, if they were honest about it. Sense of inertia having set in. One by one ticking off dreams, not because they'd been realized, but because it was understood they never would be. But that first time painting the house, that was different. Like laying fresh bets. They stood back and admired their work. Amazing what a lick of paint. Stood there silently in the quiet evening, almost afraid to move. Afraid even to breath too deeply, in case the house were only cards. Not long in love then and handled everything with exaggerated care. Later they'd eaten steak dinners and made very gentle love, as though waiting for a thing to set.

Often, after the boy dies, she stands there in the doorway and just stares, like the man does mornings, from the seat of the car. Watches the creek rise in the rain or the falling sun yellowing the field. She hears things – sounds – the ball against the house, a boy shouting. When she pushes open the door, though, there's never anybody there, and nothing bouncing down the path. Just a ghostliness to the yard, as though an empty swing were moving in the wind.

She is standing at the back door. Her body grown just thick about the middle. She is trying to recall a time when this lassitude didn't dog her. Looking out across the yard, the curve of their street, which is empty, as empty as if it had been upended and all its occupants shaken out. The air is white. March was never one thing or the other, just muted. She grabs a fistful of her flesh and shakes it like a hand.

She's thinking of those things she never should have done. If I had it to do over. What everybody says. Most likely, very little would change. She'd still have wanted them both, the man and the boy. And all else would have followed from there, just exactly as it has. She sees the boy, who isn't there any more. The jagged edge of a rock. The water, so shallow it seemed almost to mock them. She hears the echoes of games, the back and forth of two-square, chalk scratching on the sidewalk and the scuff of hopscotch. Clap in a game of jacks. Berates herself for yearning.

She tries to tell herself that nothing is all bad. That no loss is total. Even this unearthly quiet. Even the emptiness she can almost fill.

A berry passed like breath from mouth to mouth. The man's voice, thick hands, the surprising softness of his hair. Cigarettes in the morning. The seat of a car. Or in bed. Under a bridge even. The way their senses used to ache. Her thigh wedged up between his legs, her back against the wall. His form in the kitchen at dawn. Then, heading out into the rain.

If she had to define it, though, what she keeps coming back to is the graveyard. His shoes in the wet grass. How the dew shone on the tips. The soft grey felt of his fedora, tilted towards the earth. Its black band. The way the muscles in his jaw grew hard, and later, how he pounded his fists against the wall, then turned his back to it and slid to the floor. That was love, to her.

They have what you could call happiness again, gradually. Almost forgetting. You might even say a renaissance, though that was not a word they used. More the comfort of conceding the inevitable. When it came clear that they lived in each other and always would. That parting would be akin to shedding a store of essential memories. The earliest, most defining ones. The things you've always known and those brief moments when you splinter, thinking kindly of an old friend until you realize it's yourself you're thinking of.

But it was as if they had to hit bottom first. Looking too

long outside themselves for deliverance. They waited for spring which, with its birdsong and light, might reawaken them; then summer, its reminders of abandon; the catharsis of autumn; and finally, the virgin snows of mid-winter, when the nakedness outside might pare them back to their beginnings. But the accusations had begun to calcify and go without saying. And the cold between them, long since impervious to things as simple as seasons.

They spoke seldom and drank a lot most nights. He grew morose and lumbered about the half-lit house like a large brooding animal. She grew maudlin, sitting on the stoop in the darkness, sobbing and then laughing with derision at her own tears. She thought of leaving, only he did first. Just for a few days, but it was enough. He came back bleary-eyed and full of loss. She asked him questions he wasn't able to answer. There were things he couldn't quite remember. He looked nervous, like someone who's committed a crime. He swore up and down, though, that it hadn't been a woman. Just a crude brief escape. For nights he lay awake tossing, all jet-lagged from the drink.

They talked about starting over then. It was that or nothing. They sat at the table, sighing heavily, like after love. His skin looked grey and they were both too tired to fight. They felt humbled when they looked around and saw themselves. Children with their coloured blocks in heaps. Waiting to be stacked again. They talked all through the afternoon and into evening, until they were empty and exhausted. In bed that night they cradled each other, like the shocked victims of an accident. Between the two of them, not much innocence to lose.

She wonders at the way life got so crowded, so that they've had to forget a lot, as a way of clearing space for whatever's still to come. Unsure of what has or hasn't happened. Things gained and then abandoned, or so long and ardently desired, maybe never gained, but've become memories anyway. Wanting synonymous with having had.

Their own past feels so far behind them. A house they'd once inhabited, way back in the beginning, and from which they've long since moved. Grown strange and devoid of its particulars, so that they wonder was it theirs at all. They see their lives rendered in the faded hues of other decades. Colours that no longer exist.

Their future, she reckons she can picture. She has enough to go on. She knows his dreams and can be almost certain of what he will and will never do. She holds the unwelcome knowledge of his limits, and thus the outline of his demise. She can see in his shoulders the makings of a slope, his spine curving inwards at the base, belly pushed just slightly out; a body begun its slide towards the earth. She sees wood rotting, weeds growing through cracked cement, a buckled sidewalk. All sorts of picturesque decay. When there's silence, she thinks of him. She imagines him evenings, whittling on the front step, a pile of shavings at his feet. A little cedar dog, its tail raised in a permanent wag. Scenes of sweet futility.

That's the future, and she knows it could be worse. But she knows too that she'll wish for the time when they were younger, before they had limits. When they'd sat at the table, drinking tea or liquor. Passed so many nights that way. Used to talk well into the hours of the early morning. Their hands, folded, or wrapped around cups. She'd raise a finger to his lips and he'd part them. You could see in the shape of her knuckles exactly how they'd gnarl.

Pretend we're this, she'd say, and they'd make believe they were. When the night pressed pitch black against the window and they drank bourbon in the kitchen, eyeing one another across the table, like in a western. Banged down their empty glasses for effect. Cowboys, that night, steeling for some scenario they forgot to finish enacting. Got drunk instead and, laughing, staggered gently about the room, as though they were waist-deep in water. Feet roiling the sediment on the sea bed, which broke and rose in clouds around them.